*Look what people are saying about this talented author...*

Julie is known for her "flair for dialogue and eccentric characterizations."
—*Publishers Weekly*

"Funny and sassy, her books are a cherished delight."
—*Sherrilyn Kenyon*

"Kenner has a way with dialogue; her one-liners are funny and fresh. Her comic timing is beautiful, almost Jennifer Crusie-esque."
—*All About Romance*

"Hot, sexy and funny...I could not put it down."
—*Raves & Faves* on *Reckless*

_Blaze_

Dear Reader,

I love beginnings. Starting a new book, meeting new people, sitting down in a movie theater as the credits roll. It's exciting and wondrous, and all the more so when that new beginning starts contemporaneously with a whole new year full of new possibilities.

That's what I wanted for Ty and Claire—that magical wonder of something fresh and new and, in their case, jam-packed with heat and sparks and sexual energy.

I met my husband in July and got married in October (and we're coming up now on sixteen years!), so I'm a big believer in love at first sight. But that chemical rush isn't the end of the story. It's the way people—and characters—mesh their lives together that turns that initial wham-bam into something long-lasting. That's what Ty and Claire have to work on in _Moonstruck_, and I really hope you enjoy getting to know them!

Happy reading,

Julie

# Julie Kenner

## MOONSTRUCK

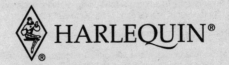

HARLEQUIN®

TORONTO • NEW YORK • LONDON
AMSTERDAM • PARIS • SYDNEY • HAMBURG
STOCKHOLM • ATHENS • TOKYO • MILAN • MADRID
PRAGUE • WARSAW • BUDAPEST • AUCKLAND

Recycling programs
for this product may
not exist in your area.

ISBN-13: 978-0-373-79518-5

MOONSTRUCK

www.eHarlequin.com

**Printed in U.S.A.**

## ABOUT THE AUTHOR

National bestselling author Julie Kenner's first book hit the stores in February 2000, and she's been on the go ever since. She has been praised by *Publishers Weekly* as an author with a "flair for dialogue and eccentric characterizations," and her books have hit bestselling lists as varied as those of *USA TODAY, Waldenbooks, Barnes & Noble* and *Locus* magazine. Julie lives in Georgetown, Texas, with her husband, two daughters and several cats.

To old friends and new ones.
Happy New Year!

# 1

CLAIRE DANIELS glanced around Decadent's crowded dance floor, with its pulsating colored lights and equally pulsating bass beat, and wondered what the devil she was doing there.

Okay, so she didn't actually *wonder*. Instead, she blamed her best friend, Alyssa, for dragging her there, dateless, on New Year's Eve.

"Blow toy?" An Adonis of a guy in a tight black T-shirt with *Decadent* stamped across it in cracked, white ghetto-style letters held something out to her, a suggestive smile on his mouth.

"Excuse me?" Claire lifted a single eyebrow in the haughty gesture that she'd perfected at the age of eight, after spending too much time watching *Star Trek* reruns, and then camping out in her bathroom until she'd been able to convince her facial muscles to move in such a way.

"For midnight," the guy said, his half-smile suggesting that he knew exactly how far into the gutter her thoughts had been. "A noisemaker."

"Oh. Right. Sure. Thanks." She snatched the gizmo, gave it an experimental toot and then smiled up at the Adonis. "Great. Thanks. This'll be fun." Her words were clipped and rushed, designed to get him to go away so that she could get back to her originally scheduled misery at being alone, in a bar, on New Year's Eve. The date night to rival all date nights.

Honestly, she shouldn't have come.

Adonis-boy melted into the crowd, and Claire scanned the room, looking for Alyssa so that she could tell her friend she'd had enough and she was going to go home. At least at home she could cuddle under a blanket and get all comfy in sweatpants. At least at home, she wouldn't feel like an idiot come midnight when everyone else was locked in a passionate kiss, and she was standing around twiddling her thumbs.

Alyssa, however, was nowhere to be found. But, frankly, that wasn't terribly troubling. Because what Claire's gaze lighted upon could only be described as eye candy of the most *decadent* sort. Tall and lean, and decked out in Texas formal, his jeans just tight enough to give a woman a serious appreciation for the man underneath, and his starched white button-down still perfectly crisp despite the heat generated by the crush of bodies in the room.

Even from where she stood, she could tell that his eyes were blue, and at the moment, they were scoping out the club, as if he was a monarch surveying his kingdom. And, oh, yeah, he looked like royalty. From the way he held himself, to the rogueish, I'm-the-dude-in-charge stubble that graced his strong jawline, he was so perfect that if he were a picture Claire would swear that he'd been digitally enhanced. The man was the visual equivalent of a Ben & Jerry's overdose, rich and wonderful and utterly bad for you.

*Down, girl.*

Then again, why?

The guy was hot. He was looking her way. And she was single and, at the moment, very, very available.

She took a step in his direction only to be stymied in her quest to go after what she wanted with gusto when a burly guy in a Decadent T-shirt approached Mr. Texas Royalty. They spoke for a few minutes, and then her gorgeous fantasy of a man followed the burly guy in the opposite direction, his expression stern.

*Security,* she assumed. Which meant that Texas Royalty was either working security, too, or he'd just been kicked out of the club.

Either way, it did her no good. If he was security, he was working. And if he was kicked out… Well, she was primed for a wild night with a hot man, but she *was* hoping to keep her crazy fling on the semi-responsible side. Hooking up with guys who got kicked out of dance clubs was not on her list of top ten smart things to do.

Too bad. Mr. Texas Royalty was seriously easy on the eyes. And right then, dammit, yes, she wanted a man. Wanted to get up close and personal. Wanted to work off some of the sexual frustration that had been building and building since she'd broken up with Joe. It had been months and months since she'd gotten naked with anyone other than her handheld shower-head, and she was really craving a man's touch right now.

*You could have had one, Claire.*

She grabbed a Jell-O shot from a passing wait-ress, then snarfed it back, snorting. Oh, yeah. She could have had a man, all right. *Joe.* Her ex. The man who'd dumped her after almost a year of dat-ing, and then—when she'd foolishly called and sug-gested they have a drink, just to see if there was any way back for the two of them—he'd suddenly de-cided that sex was a great little reconciliation tool.

And stupid her, she'd almost—*almost*—fallen

into bed with him. Then her self-respect had kicked in, and she'd marched out, not even bothering to slam the door behind her, leaving Joe looking baffled, his pants down around his ankles.

*Yeah, well, buddy. Next time think about that before you dump me.*

On the morally superior side of the equation, she was feeling pretty good about herself. On the sexually primed and then denied side of the equation, she been as taut as a wire ever since and wondering if maybe she hadn't punished herself as much as she'd punished him.

"You did the right thing." That from Alyssa, materializing beside her holding a flute of champagne, which she passed to Claire, who took it gratefully, despite being able to still taste the Jell-O from the shot she'd just downed.

"Is it that obvious what I'm thinking?"

Her friend smiled. "Only because I know you so well."

Claire sighed, then took a sip of her champagne. "It's not fair, you know. We make a Christmas pact to go after what we want—" She lifted the flute, sloshing a little as she pointed to Alyssa. "And we both know that what we wanted was men. And you end up with the man of your dreams, and I ended up with Joe, his pants around his ankles and me rushing out the door."

"Who says it had to be a *Christmas* pact? This is still the holiday season, right? You've still got time." Her grin was pure mischief.

"Easy for you to say. You're now firmly entrenched in coupledom."

"Is that what you want?"

Claire shrugged. Wasn't that the question of the hour? "Maybe not tonight," she admitted. "Tonight, I'd be happy for third base in the backseat of a car."

Alyssa laughed. "Been a while?"

"It's my own fault. I didn't have to walk out on Joe."

"Yeah," Alyssa said. "You did."

"You're right." The truth was, Claire never should have called Joe in the first place. Yes, she'd told everyone she'd been devastated by the breakup, but she'd been more devastated by the fact that her plans for a family and a future had been so rudely shattered than by the departure of that particular man. Because it was the family—the roots—that she wanted. She'd bought a house. She chaired two Dallas charity organizations. And her career was solidly on track.

She'd spent the past two years working for Judge Doris Monroe of the Fifth Circuit Court of

Appeals, and she'd recently accepted a position in the prestigious appellate law section of Thatcher and Dain. The job was bittersweet, actually, because she couldn't imagine a better boss than Judge Monroe. The woman was not only a brilliant lawyer, she was a savvy woman, and Claire respected the hell out of her. Hard to believe that in July, she'd be leaving the judge and entering the private sector.

Her father, a Texas state senator, had wanted her to join the firm that he'd helped found before he'd entered politics back when she was a little girl, but Claire was determined to make her mark on her own. If she joined a firm where her name was already on the door, it would be after she'd argued cases in front of the Supreme Court, been profiled in the *American Bar Journal* and the *Dallas Morning News,* and could walk through the front door knowing that she deserved to be there for what she'd accomplished, not because of who her dad was.

All in all, Claire was settled in her world. She just wanted someone to share it with. Joe, however, wasn't that guy, no matter how much she'd tried to pretend otherwise.

Still, hearth and home was nice, but right then—on New Year's Eve—she'd be happy with a slow dance and a hot kiss. And she'd be even happier with more.

She sighed and swallowed the rest of the champagne in her flute. "Where's Chris?" she asked Alyssa, referring to Alyssa's best-friend-turned-boyfriend-turned-man-of-her-dreams.

"He bumped into a friend. I should probably go find him, though. Only fifteen minutes to midnight."

Claire frowned. "I think I'll just go."

"Don't you dare. Just have fun. Kiss the bartender. Dance. Drink champagne."

"Oh, believe me," Claire said. "I'm all over that champagne plan." She didn't usually drink much, but between boredom and nerves, she'd drunk at least three glasses—not counting the tasty Jell-O shots—and she was feeling it, too.

"I shouldn't even be here," Claire continued. "My mother begged me to drive down to Austin and go to the celebration at the Governor's Mansion. I could be mingling with judges. Making contacts. Networking." She sighed. "Seriously. I should just go home."

"What about our pact? You need to step to it, girl. Go after what you want."

"Maybe what I want is to get in bed with a glass of wine and watch *When Harry Met Sally*."

Alyssa's expression turned stern. "For one

thing," she said, with a nod to the champagne flute, "you do not need to be driving right now. For another, it's New Year's Eve!"

"Hello? Midnight on New Year's without a date is no fun. Neither was Christmas," she added, though she wasn't bitter. Really she wasn't. She was thrilled Alyssa and Chris had finally gotten together. Claire just wished their pre-Christmas take-control-of-your-love-life holiday pact had worked out as well for herself.

"I'd let you kiss Chris, but I'd just end up being jealous," Alyssa said with a wink. "Can't have that."

Claire gave her friend a small shove in the direction of the bar. "Go. Find him. I'll be fine. Maybe I'll accost some poor, helpless man and make him be my sex slave for the evening," she added, thinking of Mr. Texas Royalty, aka The One That Got Away.

"There you go. That's the spirit." She gave Claire a quick hug, then disappeared into the throng, leaving Claire feeling like a bit of an idiot standing there all alone with the clock about ready to start counting down.

"Damn," Claire said, wondering if Alyssa would notice if she went out and sat in her car. She could pretend like she needed something, wait in the car while the clock tolled midnight, then come back in after the kissing was over. That, at least, would save her from the intense depression associated with chronic datelessness.

Armed with a plan, she stepped out of a nearby door and found herself not in front of the club but on a flagstone back patio. Moreover, the inside music was not pumped outside. Instead, there was a nice classical thing going on that gave the little oasis a "kick back and regroup" kind of feel that Claire appreciated.

As far as she could tell, though, there was no way to move from the patio to the parking lot, and she was about to turn and go back inside when she caught another glimpse of Mr. Sin-and-Sex. This time, though, he was chatting with a cluster of gorgeous women. *Figures.* She sighed, and was debating whether she should go over and count herself among the groupies, when the cluster of women broke apart and started moving off in various directions, their parting creating a straight line of sight between her and Texas—and he was staring right at her, the heat in his eyes positively unmistakeable.

*Whoa.*

She drew in a breath, then snagged another flute of champagne from a passing waiter. She turned away, not wanting Texas to see the big gulp she took for courage, realizing as she did that she was desperately out of practice on the flirting front. She'd dated Joe, yes, but she'd met him through a friend of a friend, no cold-meet in a crowded bar. And before that...well, she'd always been the girl who studied, not the girl who partied.

Now she was regretting that deficit in her education, because somehow she was going to have to find the know-how to walk right over there and talk to the man. Go after what she wanted, right? Wasn't that what she and Alyssa had agreed?

And at the moment, there was no denying that if there was anyone she wanted by her side at midnight, it was Mr. Decadant.

When she turned back around she was invigorated, self-confident...and completely alone.

Or not entirely alone, as there were several dozen people out on the patio with her, but the man she was aiming for was gone.

Well, damn.

"Not a good time to lose your date."

Claire whipped around, which set her head to spinning from the champagne, and found herself facing an absolutely gorgeous blond girl holding yet another tray, this one with both champagne and Jell-O shots. "I'm sorry? My date?"

"You have that 'where the heck did he go now?' look in your eye."

"Oh!" Claire glanced around, positively mortified that she'd had anything remotely resembling a date-look on her face with regard to a perfect stranger—even if she had been thinking about some very datish activities. "No, see, I was just—"

"The countdown's starting soon," the waitress said. "Find him quick."

And before Claire could explain to this woman who undoubtedly didn't care that the hunka hunka burning decadence was not her date, the waitress pressed a flute into her hand and flitted off to foist celebratory beverages on the rest of the unsuspecting guests.

Claire sighed. And, since she had it, she took another drink. Then she looked around the patio some more. No luck.

Of course, that really didn't mean anything. The patio was starting to get incredibly crowded, and when Claire tilted her head back like some of the other club-goers, she realized why: the full moon hung in the sky, showering the guests in moonlight.

And then she realized that the music from inside the club had stopped, as had the orchestral music that had been playing on the patio, all replaced instead by the warm voice of Fred, who introduced himself as Decadent's manager. "From me and every one of us here at Decadent, we want to wish you all a happy New Year. Now, grab your date and a get ready to toast, because we are only thirty seconds away from midnight!"

There was a shuffle as a few people reached for a fresh glass, then the crowd started counting down from fifteen, with Fred leading the way over the loudspeaker. Because she thought it might get her in the mood, Claire joined in, lifting her glass and sloshing a bit of champagne with each passing second until they were finally to—

"Four!" She took a sip.

"Three!" She glanced over as the crowd parted.

"Two!" She saw Joe. *Joe.* And he was with a date. A date! Not that she cared who he went out with—and maybe she was reverting to junior high—but she did not want him to see her there alone when he had a woman on his arm.

"One!" *And Joe saw her, too.*

*Well, hell.*

She turned away—with any luck, maybe he hadn't really seen her after all—and smacked right up against Mr. Texas Royalty.

Maybe it was the champagne. Maybe it was entrepreneurial spirit. Maybe it was a big "screw-you" to Joe. Or maybe it was the devil dancing on her shoulder. Claire didn't know. All she knew was that she looked into his clear blue eyes, put her hands on his shoulders, lifted herself up on her toes and kissed him.

SHE KISSED HIM, she thought a second later, though how her brain was functioning, Claire really didn't know. She had actually pushed herself—and her lips—off on a man.

And not just any man, but her hunka hunka burning Texas.

And not only had she kissed him, but he'd kissed her back.

Was *kissing* her back, because although her mind was spinning, the kiss was going on and on, and it was delicious. It was incredible. It was six ways to wow and back again.

And if Joe was watching, well, that was even better, because if Claire knew one thing for certain, Joe had never kissed like this. Firm, yet soft in all the right places. With just a hint of tongue and the taste of champagne and chocolate and strawberries.

With a little sigh, she opened her mouth, giving him better access, which he instantly took advantage of. His tongue swept inside her mouth, as if he wanted nothing more than to taste every inch of her, and her body seemed to dissolve on a sigh, rendering her utterly boneless and totally at his mercy.

Not a problem, though, because he was so aptly holding her up. One hand at the back of her head, his fingers thrust into the wild curls of the hair she'd let hang loose. The other at the small of her back, his fingers down, the tips grazing the curve of her rear, the sensation uncommonly erotic.

He increased the pressure with his hand, urging her closer until they were hip to hip and—*oh, sweet heaven*—she could feel the effect she was having on him pressing hard against her. *Very* hard against her, and though she knew that she ought to be embarrassed, or at least ease back so they could both get a little air, she did just the opposite, curving her body close to his and feeling the welcoming pressure as his hand slid down to settle firmly on her rear and ease her even closer, even tighter against him.

Yes, yes, oh, for the love of all that is holy, *yes.*

She shifted, imagining his hand moving lower. Imagining his fingers tracing their way down the curve of her rear then sliding between her legs, cupping her crotch. Touching her. Teasing her. Making her come.

And, oh, my God, she could feel herself getting wet

just from the very thought of his touch. What on earth would it be like if his hands actually were on her that way? If she really did have the man in her bed?

*Oh, sweet heaven, yes.*

Call it chemistry, call it champagne, call it the Fates playing with the hearts of mortals, but right then she couldn't think of anything except getting him in bed, getting him inside her. The room was spinning, and he was the only thing that was steady. The only thing that she wanted.

And then, damn the whole world, he was pulling away, gently, softly, just enough to break the kiss, and the heat she saw in his eyes just about did her in. *Oh, yeah. He'd go there with her.*

"Happy New Year to you, too," he said, with a crooked grin.

"It's shaping up to be a good one."

"I saw you," he said, in the kind of voice that only fantasy men have, smooth like a radio star, but without the salesman quality. A voice that could murmur all night to a woman in bed. A voice that could make her come without even a single touch.

"Did you?" She was melting. She was positively, undeniably melting.

"In the bar. I saw you. You saw me, too."

"Yes," she said, moving a step closer, closing the

distance that had opened between them when he'd broken the kiss. *Kiss me. Kiss me again.*

"What were you thinking when you were watching me?" He reached out, then gently pressed his hand to her waist, urging her even closer as the electricity between them snapped and popped.

She swallowed, her eyes on those lips, remembering the touch of them. The feel of them. She knew exactly—erotically—what she was thinking at the moment. The past, though…well, the past was hazy. "I—I'm having a hard time getting my brain to function."

"Are you? Because I know what I was thinking…"

"You do?" The question came out on a breath, soft and wispy and full of unabashed longing.

"This," he said, and then he tilted his head over her. And as the silver moon shined down upon them, he pressed his lips to hers and gave her the kiss she'd been wishing for.

# 2

*EXQUISITE.*

Ty could barely think because of the spell cast by the woman in his arms, and Ty Coleman wasn't the kind of man who got caught up in a spell. No, the man *Entertainment Weekly* had labeled the "Crown Prince of the Nightclub Scene"…the man who'd left his Dallas home at the age of nineteen to make his fortune in Los Angeles…the man responsible for the five most popular nightclubs in the L.A. area, and who had hosted two After Oscars parties with beautiful actresses on his arm…that man was not a man who often found himself blown away by a woman.

This woman, though…

Something about her had caught his eye.

And it wasn't her looks, although there was nothing lacking in that department, with her soft brown curls and doe-shaped eyes that were both soft and inquisitive, it was something else entirely. A sparkle. A pop. Not to mention the arc of electricity that had shot between them whenever he'd looked her direction.

He'd been certain that she'd felt it, too, which was why he'd risked his life to navigate the crowd as midnight approached simply to get near to her.

He'd caught his first glimpse of her when she'd been talking with her friend, and the way she stood— self-confident and straight despite obviously feeling out of place—had piqued his interest. He should have simply noted her and forgotten her. Lord knew he met and saw hundreds of women every night. But she'd compelled him enough to not only have him noticing, but to have him actually saying a silent thank you for the circumstances that had dragged his reluctant ass back to this Texas hellhole.

He hadn't wanted to come back. Why would he? It was one hell of a lot harder to hear his parents' constant rumbling that he'd never amount to anything from fifteen hundred miles away. Here, with them only a few miles down the highway, the sound of their discouragement was almost deafening. As if they could only see the dyslexic boy he used to be—the cocky kid who made it a point to make friends since he couldn't make good grades. Who got in fights with the boys and compromising positions with the girls. His school counselors had la-

beled him a troublemaker who wouldn't apply himself, and his parents had agreed. At least as much as
they ever agreed on anything. And even when Ty
moved to California and applied the hell out of
himself, they still only saw the useless cutup.

And damn him all to hell for still caring.

But he did. Might not want to, but he still gave
a damn, and that was why he'd always believed that
there was nothing in the world that would make
him return to Dallas.

Of course, he'd never imagined Roberto Murtaugh,
either. But when this year's Academy Award winner
for best actress had introduced Ty to the Dubai-based
billionaire at a Hollywood party, Ty had heard opportunity knocking loud and clear. He might not be able
to read a balance sheet without the numbers twisting
and turning and floating off the page, but he damn sure
knew how to make those numbers grow. He'd sat
Murtaugh down and outlined everything he'd accomplished during his years in Los Angeles. From starting
out at nineteen as a hungry entrepreneur who worked
in every club that would hire him, to the day they cut
the ribbon at the grand opening of his fifth club.

Not surprisingly, Murtaugh had heard of Ty.
Even in Los Angeles, when a guy as young as Ty
starts raking in as much money as he was making—

when he spins the success of his brick-and-mortar clubs into Internet social-networking sites—the media takes notice. At first he was dubbed the Boy Wonder, but by the time he'd been in the business a few years and had reached his twenty-eighth birthday, they'd taken to simply tagging him with a party-boy moniker. Tabloid fodder, with his frequent starlet dates and high-end lifestyle.

That was all right with Ty. The more the spotlight shined on him, the more popular his clubs became. And the truth was, he had absolutely no intention of changing the way he lived. His nightlife lifestyle had dragged him up from abject poverty, earned him more than his fifteen minutes on *Good Morning America,* started the press buzzing about him, and brought Hollywood royalty knocking on his door, asking for tickets and passes to special events and crowded nights.

If that meant he had to be labeled a party guy, then he could handle the title, even now at the age of thirty.

For that matter, he was willing to put up with whatever it took to keep growing his business. To be the guy his parents were so certain he could never be. Successful. Wealthy. Respected.

Apparently, 'whatever it took' included moving back to Dallas.

He'd hit it off with Murtaugh, but the billionaire's bankroll hadn't filled up by trust alone. And when Ty pitched Murtaugh his idea of expanding Ty's celestially named nightclubs into Europe and Asia, the investor had been both interested and wary.

"I like you," the older man had said. "But you have proven yourself only in one city. How do I know you have the spark to make this work?"

"I do," Ty had said. "Tell me how to convince you, and I'll do it."

"I have two properties," Murtaugh had said. And then he'd smiled and told Ty exactly what he wanted. Simple enough. Ty had eight months to whip one of Murtaugh's nightclubs, Decadent, into shape. Work with the staff. Consult. Do whatever magic needed to be done. And at the same time, Ty was supposed to bring to life a currently boarded-up establishment that Murtaugh was considering selling. A butt-ugly property that hadn't ever turned a profit. He and Murtaugh had agreed to a fifty-fifty split, and the property would launch as an offshoot of Heaven, Ty's very first and most popular California nightclub.

Assuming both properties got off the ground and were in the black within Murtaugh's rather insane time frame, Murtaugh promised he'd bankroll Ty's expansion.

It was, Ty thought, too good to be true.

And as soon as Murtaugh had told him the location of the properties, Ty saw the big old trick the universe was playing on him.

Accomplish his biggest dream—become the Wolfgang Puck or Gordan Ramsey of the club scene—but walk through hell first to do it.

Of course he'd said yes.

He'd been in Dallas for about six months now, and had two left on his sentence. And he couldn't wait to get the hell out of this damned town.

He forced the thoughts out of his head. It didn't matter. None of it mattered. He was there now, in the club, and for at least a few minutes, the woman in his arms was making the fact that he was stuck there significantly more pleasant.

From the moment he'd first seen her, he'd planned to go over and talk to her. Take her back to the VIP section of the club. Buy her a drink. Ask her to dance.

Never once had he imagined that she'd throw herself into his arms and kiss him like she meant it. Like she wanted it.

She moaned a little, her soft body pressing close to his. He could taste the champagne on her lips, and he'd watched her down at least a couple of flutes full as she'd scoured the place, searching for someone. A someone not him, though he had to admit that the idiot's loss was most definitely his gain.

He felt hot, needy and he wanted to touch her. Not simply the way he was touching her now, but all of her. He wanted to feel her skin beneath his fingers, slide his palms over her bare breasts. Close his mouth over her nipples and feel them harden as his tongue licked and stroked.

He wanted, and if there was one thing Ty usually made sure of, it was that he got what he wanted.

At the moment, frankly, he wanted his private office. Unfortunately, he'd never set up an office at Decadent since his role here was that of consultant. Instead, he'd rented a small office in the Wardman Towers downtown, and downtown was much too far away for his current purposes.

But, damn, he wished it weren't. Because no matter who'd been on her mind when she'd first stepped into Decadent, right now, the woman in his arms was all about him. Or she was until—

"Claire?"

The male voice came from his left, and the woman in Ty's arms, aka Claire, pulled gently away, her eyes wide, her expression wary.

"Oh. Joe. What a surprise seeing you here."

Of course it wasn't a surprise, as Ty could easily see.

"I saw you across the room. Thought I should come over and say hi."

"Right." Claire's smile was of the overly polite variety. "That's great." Her hands fluttered, as if she wasn't entirely sure what to do with them. "Happy New Year."

"You, too." He turned to Ty, his hand held out in greeting. "Ty Coleman, it's a pleasure to meet you. I'm Joe Powell," he said, holding out his hand. "Power Publicity."

Ty shook the man's hand, flipping through the Rolodex of names he kept in his mind. He'd learned a long time ago that he couldn't rely on jotted notes, and he'd trained himself to remember names and faces. *This* name, he recognized. Joe Powell had the reputation of being one of the most up-and-coming PR men in Texas, and he was on Ty's mental list of people he wanted his assistant to call to schedule a meeting. He had a feeling he wasn't going to have to bother Lucy with that now—unless he missed his guess, Joe Powell hadn't come over to see Claire, but to introduce himself to Ty.

"Listen," Joe said, "I'm not the type who plays coy, and the truth is, I came here tonight hoping to meet you."

*Bingo,* Ty thought, then noted Claire's confused expression. Joe might know who he was, but Claire was clueless. The realization surprised and pleased him, because he couldn't even remember the last time that a woman had been attracted solely to him, and not to the trappings that made up Ty Coleman.

Joe grinned at Claire. "I suppose I could have asked you to introduce us," he said. "I didn't realize you knew Mr. Coleman…"

"Yes, well." Her brow creased, as if she was debating what to say next.

Ty had no idea what made him do it, but he took her hand and pressed a soft kiss to her palm. "Our relationship's been a little whirlwind."

Claire opened her mouth, but didn't say anything, and Ty could practically see the debate raging across her face. Should she mention the fact that they had no relationship, or just go with the flow?

Ty was beginning to think she was about to set the record straight, when a lanky redhead with nail-point heels and a smile as big as Texas stepped forward and took Joe's hand. "I know all about whirlwind," Joe said. "This is Bonita," he said, as Claire's eyes went wide.

The girl's smile grew brighter. "I'm Joe's girl-friend."

CLAIRE'S HEAD WAS SPINNING, and she was certain it wasn't just from the champagne. For one thing, why did Joe know who Mr. Texas Royalty was? *Ty Coleman.* She stifled a small frown, because the name really did sound familiar, but with her fuzzy head, she couldn't latch on to why.

And what the devil was Joe doing with a girl-friend? Was this the same Joe who had, only a few days before Christmas, made a huge pass at her?

Then again, it had been Bonita who'd used the *G*-word, not Joe, so maybe the girl was posturing?

Claire considered that, then firmly shoved the thought out of her mind. Honestly, what did it matter if Bonita was his girlfriend or his fiancée or even his mail-order bride? Right then, she simply wanted both of them to leave. She didn't know why Ty was of any interest to Joe, but she did know that he was of serious interest to her. And she wanted him all to herself again.

Apparently, there was power in positive thinking, because Joe took a step backward, as if he was about to leave. Claire did a little mental happy dance, then stumbled when Bonita caught his arm. "You should invite them, sugar."

"Honey, I'm sure now's not the time," he said, although Claire knew him well enough to know that Joe never missed an opportunity to schmooze a potential client, and for a moment, she wondered if he and Bonita had scripted the invitation—whatever it was for.

"I'll have my office call and arrange a meeting with Mr. Coleman next week," Joe went on. "Would that be okay?" he asked Ty. "I'd love to talk to you about publicity for the grand opening of Heaven. I know you've been using someone else for this place, but I really think that Power Publicity has the contacts and the know-how to help Heaven make a huge splash. And now that you're a month away from opening, it's time for us to take a hard look at your PR plan. My goal for you would be to have Heaven, Dallas, open even bigger, stronger and flashier than any of your California clubs."

It was, Claire thought, a total V-8 moment. "You're Ty Coleman," she blurted, which she wouldn't have done without the champagne. "Of course!"

"You didn't—" Joe began.

"Private joke," Ty said. "When we first met, she didn't realize who I was."

"Awww," Bonita said, apparently charmed.

"Give my office a call," Ty said to Joe. "Tell my assistant I said to set up thirty minutes. If I like what I hear, we'll go from there."

"Sounds great," Joe said, looking like a man who'd just won the lottery. "Looking forward to it."

"Why don't you invite them to the party?" Bonita said.

Joe's gaze darted to Claire. "Oh, I don't know—"

"Why on earth not? I know Daddy would love to meet Mr. Coleman, and you two would have the chance to get to know each other without all that business stuff. Besides," she said, with a bright smile toward Claire, "it'll be nice having someone else around who's not in PR. You're not, are you?"

"Appellate law," Claire said. "Who's your father?" she asked, though she had a feeling she already knew.

"Jake Powers. He owns the company Joe works for." She gave Joe's arm a squeeze. "He's just invited Joe to be a partner."

"That's great," Claire said, even while a mean little side of her wondered if that was why Joe had dumped her—so he could date Bonita and get closer to Daddy. Or maybe Claire had just grown up in a political family, and saw those kind of machinations everywhere she looked.

"You'll come, right?"

"When is it?" Ty asked.

"Tomorrow. It's our annual New Year's Day client-appreciation bash at the Starr Resort. It's very casual. Come and go."

The idea of a party—with Joe—was really not on Claire's top-ten list of things to do on the first day of a new year. "I really don't think—"

"It's going to be fabulous," Bonita said. "Several of your breed, too. We've just signed with Daniels and Taylor to do some television spots," she added, referring to the law firm that Claire's father had helped found. "And I know at least five representatives from the local Bar Association are coming, along with dozens and dozens of attorneys. You never know who you might meet."

Claire lifted a brow. "And you don't work there?"

"Me? Lord, no. But I keep an eye out for the men in my life." Her smile widened. "Now come on, you two. It's not as if you have to stay all day."

Claire hesitated, balancing the possibility of networking against the reality of being at a party with Joe. In the end, networking won out. How could it not? An appellate lawyer's clients were other lawyers. And it was never too early to start honing those connections.

Beside her, Ty slid his arm around her waist, the contact making Claire tremble with the anticipation of getting them alone again. More than that, of getting the man himself for a whole day tomorrow. But as that thought entered her head, Claire knew she was being ridiculous. For one thing, a hot kiss on New Year's Eve didn't necessarily translate into a wild night—or a well-mannered daytime date. And that was probably especially true with a man like Ty Coleman. Claire didn't regularly pay attention to celebrity-type gossip, but she'd seen enough to know that Ty was the kind of guy who had a different girl on his arm in every picture that was snapped.

Maybe he wanted a night with her—and, yes, she sure as hell hoped he did—but the odds that he wanted it to continue into anything beyond that were absolutely beyond slim.

It was an utterly depressing thought, all the more so when she realized that she really couldn't go to the party without him. Because it wasn't her that Joe was interested in. Not personally, and not with regard to his PR campaign. Which meant that she'd feel like a total idiot going to this party if Ty didn't go with her. And considering she'd just met the guy, really, what were the chances of that?

"The truth is, I'd love to," Claire said, deciding to take the easy, polite way out. "But I'm afraid I have plans tomorrow."

"*We* had plans," Ty said, in a voice that had her conjuring all sorts of fantasies. He slid his arm around her waist, and she about melted on the spot. "But don't you remember?" he added, his mouth dangerously close to her ear. "We ended up canceling. Our schedule is wide-open tomorrow."

She looked at him with surprise and optimism, and caught the quick wink that he sent her, along with a mischievous quirk of his mouth. Then he turned back to face Joe and Bonita, his smile bright. "Thanks so much for the invitation. We'd love to come."

# 3

"NOT THAT I'M UNHAPPY with the outcome, but what if I'd really had plans?" They were sitting at the bar, and Ty had his hand on her knee, his fingers just barely under the hem of her skirt. Ostensibly casual, but the effect was anything but, and Claire was having a hard time concentrating, much less breathing.

"Did you have plans?"

"Well, I was supposed to go to the hospital and donate a kidney, but I guess I won't be doing that anymore."

He leaned closer, then pressed his hand flat against her lower belly. "Anyone would be lucky to get your kidney." His words were teasing, but she didn't smile. How could she when she could barely think. Her whole body was tense. His touch, his smell, even the soft sound of his breath was absolutely driving her crazy, and it was taking every ounce of effort not to close her hand over his on her belly and move it up to her breast, then slide his hand on her thigh up, up to where she really wanted to feel it.

Oh, dear Lord, she wanted to feel it. *Him.* His hands all over her. And right then, the biggest question on her mind was why, why, *why* were they still sitting in that bar?

He lifted his hand from her stomach, and she managed to breathe again. He signaled for the bartender to bring them another round, then he took her hand in his. "I thought I was doing you a favor. Did I assume wrong?"

She licked her lips. "I was that obvious?"

"I've learned to watch people. I spend a lot of time negotiating. People don't usually say what they're thinking."

"What was I thinking?" She wondered if he could tell that she'd been fantasizing about a day with him and, yes, she wondered if he wanted that, too.

"You were thinking the party sounded like an opportunity."

"It is." She sounded defensive, and she tried to tone it back. "I mean, I've been working for a judge for a while now. Great experience, great credentials, but I need to make my own contacts. I'm moving into private practice this summer."

"No need to justify yourself to me. I'm a man who survived and thrived chasing opportunities."

She tried to remember what she'd heard about him. She'd seen his name before when she turned on various celebrity gossip shows, and those types of programs seemed to be all over the television lately. And every once in a while she saw a reference on a blog. She didn't tend to follow that kind of stuff, so the fact that she'd even once bounced up against his name suggested that he really was tabloid fodder, and if Joe was chasing after him, then Ty's clubs must be some of the hottest around.

"Well, I appreciate it. It was you they really want to come, not me." She frowned. "Frankly, I'm surprised Joe didn't make more of an effort to keep me from coming." She frowned, wondering if she should say something to Bonita when she saw her the next day, then decided it depended on whether Joe had already started dating Bonita when he'd made his pass at her. She'd have to find out.

"You're looking pensive," he said, picking up the scotch that the bartender had set in front of him and taking a sip. "Want to share?"

"No," she said with a laugh. "I really don't, and yet here I am running my mouth off with you."

He dragged the tip of his finger along the edge

of his glass, making it wet with condensation. Then he drew his fingertip slowly over her lips. "I happen to like your mouth," he said in a tone that really should only be used in bed while naked.

She closed her eyes, soaking up the sound of his voice, then drew his finger in, tasting him, a hint of scotch, a dash of musk and one-hundred percent male.

She heard a little moan and realized it was coming from her.

She opened her eyes and saw that he was smiling at her, the heat in his eyes unmistakeable. To her surprise, she didn't feel embarrassed. Instead, she felt sexy. Strong. "I think you're making me a little crazy."

"Maybe it's the champagne," he said.

She shook her head. "The champagne may account for some of the courage, but it's the man who's making me—"

"Yes?"

*Wet.* "Itchy."

"Maybe I can help you scratch the itch."

Her breath hitched in her throat. "I really wish you would."

His smile was practically edible, and as he leaned in, she knew she wanted to taste it. Wanted to consume it, and when his lips brushed hers, she slid hungrily into the kiss, lips only at first, then leaning closer, her arm hooking around his neck as she lost herself in the wonder that was this man. This *heat.*

The rough sound of a clearing throat caught their attention, and Ty pulled away, breaking the kiss slowly and then, Claire was glad to see, looking at their interloper with an expression that suggested the interruption better be worth it.

The culprit was a girl, probably in her early twenties, wearing a tight Decadent T-shirt, and from the way she was grinning, she felt not the slightest bit of remorse for interrupting. As if Claire was just another girl, and this was just another night with clubster Ty Coleman.

*Well, that's probably true. Is that a problem?*

He leaned in and kissed her hard enough to make her melt, then met and held her eyes, his hot enough to melt steel.

*Nope,* she thought. *No problem at all.*

"I'm sorry," he said, sliding off the stool, his hand sliding along her thigh as he moved, and sending a shiver down her spine and shooting a promise between her legs. "I need to go run over a few closing details with Fred. Wait for me?"

She nodded, feeling a little dizzy, a lot girlie, and remarkably like she had the night that Tommy

Blake—her teenage crush—had kissed her under the bleachers for the very first time.

Lost in her thoughts, she pulled a cherry out of one of the bar dishes and started to suck on it, her gaze sweeping casually over the room. She saw Joe and Bonita heading for the door, and quickly turned away, not wanting to meet their eyes. When she did, she found Alyssa, hidden with Chris in a throng that was moving for the far door. Alyssa whispered something to Chris, who shot Claire a friendly wave as Alyssa headed in her direction.

"I was going to fire off a text message," Alyssa said, "but since you're alone now…" She trailed off, then bit her lower lip. "*Are* you alone now?"

"Only temporarily," Claire said, feeling slightly giddy.

"He's gorgeous," Alyssa said, taking Ty's seat. "See? What did I tell you about sticking around? What's he like? What's his name?"

"He's great," Claire said. "So far, anyway. And his name's Ty." She paused a bit, to see if Alyssa would react. "Ty Coleman."

"Great name," her friend said, and Claire wasn't sure if she should be impressed with herself for having more pop culture knowledge than Alyssa, or ashamed.

"Does he work here?" She nodded to something over Claire's shoulder, and when she turned, she saw Ty talking with the tall man who'd counted down to the New Year. He looked over while he was speaking, caught her eye and smiled.

"Bang and pop," Alyssa said.

"What?"

"The way you two are looking at each other. It's not just lust. It's a connection."

Claire laughed, brushing aside her friend's words. "You only want me to be a couple now that you are. I just met the man."

Alyssa shrugged. "Believe what you want," she said in a voice that suggested she knew what she was talking about and Claire was hopelessly ignorant. "But you definitely owe me for convincing you to stay. I was coming over to tell you that you better not be planning on driving tonight, but since it looks like you've got an escort home, I'm not going to worry about it. But," she added, as she leaned in to give Claire a hug, "don't you dare drive."

"I'll consider it a stellar excuse to go home with the man. If he wants me to," she added, the possibility that he wouldn't disturbing her more than it probably should.

"Trust me," Alyssa said, with a decidedly mischievous grin, "I'm certain he does." She wiggled her fingers and backed away before Claire could get another word out, and it was only when she felt the soft press of Ty's hand on her shoulder that she realized why Alyssa had departed so abruptly.

"Sorry about that. Technically, I'm on the clock."

"Oh. I'm sorry. I—"

"No, no," he said, taking her hand before she could do something stupid like hop off the stool and—what? Because she wasn't leaving. Not without this man. Not if she could help it. "One of the benefits of being the man in charge—I get to play by my own rules. But one of my rules is to work when work needs to be done."

"And what work needed to be done at twelve-thirty on New Year's Day?"

"More than you might think," he said, sliding back on the bar stool and leaning back, looking for all the world as if he owned the place. Actually, maybe he did own the place. "For one thing, people drink more tonight."

"So they do," she said, lifting her glass. She rarely drank champagne—primarily because it went to her head and made her sleep like the dead— but she'd been indulging wildly this evening. And now she was enjoying the effects—and the courage—that came with the nice little buzz she had going on.

"Exactly," he said, with a chuckle. "So we have to make sure that we've made arrangements with local taxi services, shuttles, whatever it takes. I've even been known to put people up at a hotel if I was afraid they'd get into their car. It's an expense, but it's worth it, and it's paid off in goodwill, particularly among the college crowd.

"And, then, of course, there's the problem of the till," he continued. "Not that an increased cash drawer is a problem, but I don't want the manager going alone to make the night deposit. Then you have the logistical issues of how to coordinate with your neighbors tomorrow morning, because inevitably someone has knocked over a corporate sign or left cigarette butts on the sidewalk. We're located in a mixed-use area, so the club is next to restaurants and retail, and they'll both be open tomorrow morning and wanting their grounds to be pristine. And then you have to deal with—"

He cut himself off with a quick shake of his head. "I'm getting a bit carried away."

"A little. Maybe. But it's interesting. I had no idea so much went into closing a club for the night.

To be honest, my experience with the nightclub environment was more or less limited to a night at the symphony with my parents. At least until college, but even then I tended to—"

"Study more than you went out?" he said.

"That obvious?"

"I'm just familiar with the breed."

"I take it you weren't a studier?"

"I made a college career out of not studying," he said, "and I mastered it so well that I got my degree in abject unstudiousness at nineteen and set out into the world to make my fortune."

"And how did you end up in our little corner of the world?"

"Full circle, it looks like. At least temporarily."

She shook her head. "I'm sorry. I don't understand."

"I was born here. Went to SMU. Learned how to dance the two-step." He bent down and tugged up his jeans, then tapped his boots. "Can't you tell," he added, adding an affectation of a Texas twang to his voice as he spoke.

"Now that you mention it. But okay, why are you back?"

"Long story," he said. "Bottom line is I'm back for two more months, and although I was dreading the fact that I had sixty full days ahead of me, now I'm thinking that my incarceration is looking much more tolerable. Not time served, but I've gotten a few perks."

"Conjugal visits?" she quipped, the words out before she even realized what she was saying. "Oh…I…"

"Don't you dare," he said, that ribbon of heat she'd felt earlier flowing back into his voice. "Don't you dare take that back." He took a cherry out and passed it to her, dangling it so that it grazed her lower lip. She opened her mouth to take it, and he pulled it just out of reach. She laughed, then leaned forward, her hand going out to steady her, and finding purchase on his stool, right between his legs.

She caught the cherry and drew it in, closing her eyes as she suckled it. He shifted, and she felt the warmth of his inner thighs at her fingertips, then opened her eyes to see that her hand was right there—right next to the bulge in his jeans. So close that all she had to do was shift her fingertips to touch him, or move her hand to cup him. She imagined what would happen if he touched her that way—if his hand dipped down and cupped her, finding her wet, sliding a finger inside, closing his mouth over hers as he made her come.

*Oh, dear.*

It was in her head now. This need to touch him.
To stroke him. To make him as absolutely crazy as
his mere proximity was making her, and without
thinking, she shifted her hand only slightly, then
stroked him through his jeans. She felt him twitch
under her touch, saw the way his body stiffened, and
heard the slow, rough intake of his breath. She
leaned in closer, feeling sexy and powerful, then
lifted her head to face him. "Kiss me," she demanded, then lost herself in the sweet pleasure of
an obedient man who did exactly, positively, totally,
what she asked.

As his mouth drew her in, making her head
spin and her body tingle, his hand stroked her
back, bare from the halter-style dress she wore.
His touch was intimate, possessive, and Claire's
mind was fuzzy with lust. In most fairy tales, the
girl turned back into herself at the stroke of midnight. Claire's personal fairy godmother, however,
apparently approached her job from an inverted
perspective. Because on the stroke of midnight,
Claire had transformed from being Dateless
Claire, to being Claire-with-the-gorgeous-guy.

And not just any gorgeous guy, but a guy who
seriously knew how to kiss. And how to make her

laugh. True, the champagne was probably adding to the fizzy, floaty mood, but the real reason was Ty. The way he talked. The way he laughed.

And, oh, yes, the way he kissed. Like right now. Like he couldn't get enough. Like he wanted to wrap her up and take her home and trail kisses down to the kinds of places that didn't get kissed on bar stools.

Just the thought made her squirm, trying to find a position where the heat building between her thighs didn't make her crazy. That, however, was impossible. Might as well admit it—she was tipsy, turned on and totally hot for the guy. And if she didn't get him into a bed soon—if she didn't touch him all over the way her fingers were itching to touch him, and if she didn't feel him deep inside her making her absolutely wild—she had a feeling she *would* go crazy.

She was already half crazy as it was, and they'd done nothing but kiss.

He started to pull away, and she whimpered a protest, catching his lower lip with her teeth and softly tugging. The grin that spread to his eyes was slow and full of male pride and Claire, in full shameless hussy mode, didn't care at all, because right then she was enjoying him too much, and if he wanted to feel self-satisfied about the fact that he had totally turned her on...well, she could live with that.

"Can you leave?" she murmured, praying the answer was yes. "Or do you have work to do?"

"To hell with work," he said, sliding off the bar stool and coming to stand in front of her. An absurd wave of gratefulness swept through her, although she didn't believe him for one second. She'd heard the passion in his voice. If there was work to be done, he wouldn't abandon it. But thank God there wasn't and he was free to go.

She slid her arms around his waist, pulling him even closer to her, certain if they didn't leave soon she would spontaneously combust from the heat building inside her. "Then let's get out of here."

She slid off the bar—and the room started spinning. He hooked his arm around her waist, and she looked up at him with a combination of gratefulness and sheepishness. "Sorry. Champagne does this thing to me."

"Good thing you're with a man who makes it a point to get all the customers home safe." He brushed a featherlight kiss across her ear, making her shiver. "I promise, I'll see to it personally."

She drew in a breath, thinking about Ty in her

house. In her bed. "My house is a mess," she said softly. "It's the maid's year off."

"Maybe I should just kiss you good-night at the door, then."

She heard the tease in his voice and rose to the challenge. Reaching up, she hooked her arm around his neck, then pulled his head down to hers. With her other hand, she cupped his rear, easing him toward her until their bodies meshed and she could feel the hard length of him pressed against her, straining beneath the tight denim of his jeans. A wave of feminine power surged through her, and she lifted herself up on her toes, letting her body press up hard against his, and positioning her lips so that they just brushed his ear.

"Don't you dare," she whispered. "I want you in my bed, Ty. And the sooner, the better."

# 4

*"I WANT YOU IN MY BED."*

Damn, but Ty knew the feeling. Right then, he could barely think, what with the havoc the woman was wreaking upon him. He could feel the effect of her through every inch of his body. The pulse that beat so hard at his throat. The tingle of skin where she brushed against him. And the painful length of his cock that strained for a release that really couldn't wait for a bed.

He had no idea where she lived, but he hoped like hell it was close. *Very* close.

He thought about the room he was renting from one of his former fraternity brothers, but then remembered the two other guys who'd arrived over the last few days and were crashed in the house, as well. It was only three blocks away, but it was also the consummate bachelor pad, and definitely no place to take Claire.

He considered a hotel, but it didn't seem right. He wasn't entirely sure why—Lord knew he'd taken a lot of women to hotels at closing time over the years. He even kept a permanent room at the Chateau Marmont for exactly that reason. He didn't want to take them back to his place, and when they invited him back to theirs, it never felt right. Like by going, he was making a statement that he didn't want to be making.

With Claire, he somehow didn't mind the statement. He told himself it was because he was in Dallas with only two short months left, so why not go to her house? It wasn't as if they were going to slide into anything permanent. In sixty days, he was out of there and on a plane to Paris, with follow up-trips to London, Munich and Sydney.

Right then, though, he wasn't thinking about his foreign opportunities. He was interested only in the woman in his arms, and the truth was, unless she lived right next door, he really didn't think he could make it anywhere before his body imploded from passion and need.

"Please," she whispered, her hands warm against his ass as she pressed closer to him. Her breasts were firm against him, soft in the flimsy dress that she wore without a bra.

"Come on," he growled, making a decision. He led her through the small kitchen and into the short hallway that led through the employees-only section, then breathed a sigh of relief—when he saw that the door to his destination was open.

"Here." He didn't wait for her to answer, simply pulled her inside the small employee lounge, snapped the lock on the door, and backed her up, hard, against the wall. "Can't wait," he said, as his hands slid over her breasts.

"Thank God."

Her fingers reached for his fly, her palm first sliding up over him, pressing hard against his cock, giving him just a hint of the pleasure to come. He drew his hands up, then untied the knot that held her halter top on. The soft material tumbled down, freeing her perfect breasts.

"Claire," he murmured, realizing that, he was lost, absolutely lost. His hands stroked her back, easing around so that his thumbs could brush the swell of her breasts, even as his mouth closed around one pert nipple.

She moaned, arching toward him as she closed her eyes and tilted her head up. "Don't stop," she whispered, which was a ridiculous thing to say, really, because he had no intention of stopping.

He suckled her, his fingers easing down her back as he did so, a man on a mission. He clutched the soft material of her dress, bunching it in his hand as he slid his hand under, stroking her bare thigh up to the tender skin where her silky panties covered the prize.

She made a soft noise of pleasure, her hips moving as he explored, her hands at his back tugging free his shirt, as if she had to feel his skin beneath her hands.

Damn, but he knew the feeling.

He traced his finger over her panties, sliding it between thighs that she opened for him, shifting her stance as she moaned, her desperate cry of, "please," so soft he almost couldn't hear it.

He couldn't stop. He had to feel her. Had to hold her while she trembled and shook. Right then his whole world was about making Claire come, and he stretched his finger forward over soaking-wet panties, the feel of which made him so hard he was certain he was going to stretch his jeans out of shape. He found her clit and stroked the material, the hard little nub hidden beneath a flimsy strip of silk.

Pink, he imagined. Just like her. He wanted to see her. Wanted to taste her when she came. He wanted her to cry out, he wanted her nails digging into him as she rode out an absolutely killer orgasm.

Mostly, he wanted inside her.

"I can't wait," he said.

"Don't."

He yanked her panties down, then followed suit with his own jeans, thanking whatever guardian angel had been watching over him when he'd tucked a condom into his wallet that morning. He sheathed himself, then palmed her sex, using his middle finger to stroke her clit and tease her. "Now," she said. "Ty, please, *now.*"

Since that sounded like a damn fine idea, he turned her around, his mouth nuzzling her neck. He stroked his hands up the inside of her thighs, spreading her legs, his cock sliding over her smooth skin to find her slick, wet sex. With one hand, he stroked her breast, as with the other he guided his cock, rubbing the tip against her, almost afraid he'd come right then.

"Don't tease," she said. "Please, please don't tease."

That was all it took, and he thrust inside her, a little at first as her body stretched to accommodate him, then more and more until she completely sheathed him, and the pleasure of being inside her was like heaven times ten.

"Harder," she whispered, her hips rising and falling

as she matched his rhythm. They pistoned together, finding a natural rhythm, hard and fast, as her body closed over him, drawing him in, claiming him.

He felt it when she began to come. The tremble in her body, the way her vagina clenched around him, like a velvet fist, pumping him and hurrying him along. He thrust harder, wanting to come with her, to lose himself in the stars with her, and the soft, sweet sounds she made—small, desperate gasps of pleasure—worked on him like an aphrodisiac.

Her entire body began to tremble as the orgasm rolled over him. She squeezed him, milking him, and with one last, final thrust, he came along with her, the pleasure so intense it was a wonder he didn't pass out from it. Instead, he collapsed against her, turning her gently so that he could kiss her, stroke her, look into those gorgeous chocolate eyes. That's what she was—rich and decadent and utterly sinful.

He pulled out, but slid his finger down, teasing her clit and sending a last few shockwaves coursing through her body, the pleasure he saw in her face as he did almost enough to make him come again, too.

Finally, she exhaled—a low, shaky breath. She tilted her head back and looked up at him, her lips plump and ripe, her eyes shining. "Wow," she said, and he saw a hint of mischief in his eyes. "That was amazing. I wonder how much better we'd do with an actual bed."

He exhaled, only then realizing that he'd feared she'd be done with him. Itch scratched, time to move on. And that wouldn't work for him. His itch hadn't been scratched at all. Right then, Ty wasn't certain that he could ever have enough of this woman.

"Maybe we need to find out," he said.

She cupped her hand behind his neck then reached up to kiss him. Long and hard and demanding. A kiss with both purpose and promise. "Don't you dare leave me on my doorstep. This was an appetizer," she said, then slid her hand down to cup his cock, which twitched with definite purpose. "You come inside and we'll gorge ourselves on the main course."

"I THINK I LEFT MY PANTIES on the floor," Claire said, as they stepped outside the building and the steel fire door shut behind them. Any other night—with any other man—and that announcement would completely mortify her.

With Ty, she was simply grateful she hadn't left her dress crumpled up, as well.

"Don't worry," he said, his hand sliding down to cup her now-naked rear through the thin material of her dress. "You won't need them." His dragged his finger down her bare arm, sending shivers through her. "Do you have a coat?" The night was unseasonably warm for Dallas, but even in the high forties, backless dresses required coats, and at the moment, she didn't have one. She shivered again, his words reminding her to be cold—reminding her that there was life outside of his arms.

"I checked it," she said, automatically stopping and shifting her weight to head back inside the club.

He gently tugged her back, then took off the sport coat he'd grabbed from a peg near the back door. "Wear this. I'll see to yours tomorrow."

She slid her arms into the silk-lined sleeves, then pulled the coat tight around her, not so much for warmth, but because she wanted to breathe in the scent of Ty. "Now you're cold."

"Trust me," he said, his gaze skimming over her. "I'm anything but."

Any guilt she might have felt at usurping his coat faded when she realized the short distance they had to walk—not to mention the exceptional car they were about to get into. "Wow," she said, pressing her nose to the glass and peering into the slick red Ferrari. "Yours?"

"Actually, it's a rental," he said, clicking the remote to unlock the car. He stepped to the passenger side and held the door open for her. "I figured I deserved it."

"During your incarceration," she said, her voice light, but her heart a little heavy. Which was silly. It wasn't as if she worked for the Dallas Chamber of Commerce and had to play rah-rah girl for her town. And it wasn't as if she cared about him staying permanently. How could she? They'd barely met.

*Bang and pop.*

Alyssa's words fizzled in her mind, and she squashed them down. This was a lust thing. A passion thing. A serious-scratching-of-an-itch thing.

But still, she couldn't ignore the piece of her that wished he liked Dallas. Or at least wished he was stuck there for more than two months. *Sixty days*— it hardly seemed like any time at all.

She settled into the passenger seat, fastening the belt as she forced herself not to think about him leaving, but to instead enjoy the smell of leather and Ty and the deliciously fast car.

"I almost wish I lived farther away," she said. "Seems a shame not to take this car for a spin."

"I have a different kind of spin in mind," he said, his words making her all hot and gooey again.

"Keep talking like that and I won't need this coat anymore."

"Good," he said. "I like the way the dress shows off your curves."

"Do you?" She leaned forward and slid out of the coat, then folded it over her lap.

He tapped the brakes before turning onto the street. "No, no," he said, then pushed it off and onto the floorboard. "Don't worry," he added, in response to her raised eyebrows. "It'll dryclean." He put his hand on her leg, then slid it slowly up, his fingers dancing under the hem of the dress. Her sex throbbed. She was naked under there, and his fingers were close, so close, and—

Then they were gone, placed on the gear shift. *Damn.*

"Where do you live?"

"Turn left," she managed, silently pleading him to put his hand back. "We're going toward White Rock Lake."

His mouth curved into a crooked grin. "Right now, I'm wishing I rented an automatic."

"Hell, yes."

He shifted, then pulled onto the street. "Why don't we trade?"

"What? Me drive?" She was lousy on a standard,

and she'd be absolutely terrified she'd wreck the thing. And then there was the champagne…

"No, my insurance only covers me behind the wheel. I meant with touching you." The suggestion in his voice was unmistakeable, and she felt her pulse increase.

"Do you mean—"

"Put your hand on your thigh."

"I—"

"Shh. Trust me. And close your eyes."

She couldn't. She couldn't do what he was asking—touch herself in front of him. Close her eyes, expose her sex, make herself come. She couldn't…

Except maybe she could, because with Ty… Oh, Lord, with him, she wanted to. Wanted to be wild. Wanted to turn him on. Wanted to get them both so hot the house would catch on fire when they made love again, and—

"That's the way."

She hadn't even realized she'd complied, but her head was back, spinning slightly from the champagne still flowing through her system, and her fingertips were stroking her inner thigh.

"What—"

"No, no. No talking unless I ask you a question. What's your address?"

She told him, and she heard an electronic beep as he entered the location in a GPS system.

"Spread your legs."

She did, the wisp of air against her wet sex wonderfully erotic.

"Now put your other hand on your thigh…that's right. Just your fingertips. Let them graze that soft skin, just up and down. Do you like that?"

"Mmm-hmm," she said, not quite able to manage actual words.

"Who's touching you?"

"You."

"Do you want me to keep touching you like that?"

She moaned, because she didn't. She wanted more. She wanted it all.

"What do you want, Claire?"

"Please," she said. "I want you inside me."

"So do I." His voice was low, rough, and the sound of it made her even wetter. Without thinking, she spread her legs even more. "There you go," he said. "Now slide your right hand up your thigh. Go slow. Good girl. Do you feel it? Can you feel how wet you are?"

She couldn't answer. She could only breathe. Could only focus on the sensations washing over her. Her hand, his voice and the image in her mind that the touch was his tongue, tasting her, flicking over her clit, opening her up and making her come until the pleasure was too much to bear and crossed the line into pain.

"Slide your fingers over yourself. Are you slick? Can you feel your clit? Is it swollen? Is it desperate?"

"I want to come. Please, Ty, I want you to touch me, and I want to come."

"I am touching you. Those are my hands on you, stroking you, playing with you. You're so wet, and I'm so hard. I want to be inside you, Claire, but right now, all I want you to do is come. Can you make yourself come? Can you touch yourself, stroke yourself and—"

*Oh, sweet heavenly night.*

The orgasm positively ripped through her. She tossed her head back, her body bucking as wave after wave passed over her. She drew in ragged breaths until it passed, her eyes closed, and when it passed, she stayed there, breathing softly, not wanting the moment to end, but not wanting to look at Ty, either. Because now the embarrassment was setting in. She had to, though. She couldn't sit there, half-naked with her eyes closed, and so she when she felt the car stop for a light, she opened her eyes and turned to him slowly.

He was staring at her with such open adoration, such blatant lust, that whatever hint of embarrassment she'd felt faded instantly. "You're beautiful," he said, and she felt her cheeks burn with the compliment.

She glanced out the window and saw the familiar roads. "We're getting close."

"Thank God," Ty said, and she laughed, unable to miss the evidence of his arousal hard against his leg.

"What about my car?" she said, as the fuzz started to lift from her brain. "I parked in the restaurant next door, but the sign said they'll tow if you're there in the morning when they open."

"No worries," he said, then made a quick call on his cell phone to the club manager. "All set," he said when he clicked off the call.

She smiled, easing back into the bucket seat. "It feels nice to be taken care of. Not something I have a lot of experience with, actually."

His brow raised. "Joe didn't take care of you? Not sure I should consider giving my business to a man who doesn't know how to treat his girlfriend right."

"Was it that obvious we used to date?"

From his expression she was certain that it was.

"It's been a few months," she said. "In fact, until tonight, we'd only seen each other once." She frowned, thinking of the way he'd come on to her.

"A fight?"

"What? Oh, no. But…well, it was before Christmas, and he made a pass at me."

"Can't say I blame him. See, there's a mark in the man's favor. He has good taste."

She rolled her eyes. "What he has, is a girl-friend." The frown returned. "If they were dating back then…" She trailed off with a shrug. "I'm just wondering if I should tell Bonita."

"That Joe made a pass at you?"

"Well, yeah."

"They're not engaged."

"No."

"They seemed happy."

"Yeah."

"They're just dating. Unless they've changed the rules, until you cross certain dating lines, exclusivity is not required."

"Oh." She licked her lips, forcing herself not to frown. But he was right, and the thought depressed her. Not because she much cared what Joe was doing, but because the idea of Ty so casually thinking that going out with a woman other than Claire tomorrow would be totally fine.

She tamped down on the thoughts, because her mind was clearly honing in on a relationship despite the fact that a relationship was not on the table. "Actually, Joe's the reason we met," she said, trying to shift the conversation. "Indirectly, anyway. Since I was single on New Year's Eve, my best friend dragged me out."

"Remind me to thank her," he said.

"I already have."

"So we've established that Joe didn't adequately take care of you, the lousy bastard," he added, making her laugh. "What about before Joe? Who took care of you then?"

"Aah, my tale is one of woe and strife," she said, then added, "Just kidding," when he raised his brows. "Seriously, though, I've been on my own for a while. My parents are awesome, don't get me wrong, but they live in Austin. I went to boarding school here for high school, and then college, too. SMU, as well," she added, with a smile. "See, we've got something in common."

"Why boarding school?"

"My dad's a Texas state senator, and my mom's a consultant with an international consortium. She travels all the time, and so it just made sense. They're in Paris right now. Or maybe Kenya." She frowned, then shook her head. "Honestly, I just keep their schedule in my PDA. It's too hard to keep in my head. At any rate, they've always traveled like that. Together when Daddy can get away, or Mom by herself when he can't. So I was shipped here. I loved it, though. And I ended up loving Dallas, too, which is why I've stayed. Well, that and the fact that I wanted to make it on my own. When you have parents like mine, it's almost inevitable that nepotism will be involved. I didn't want it to be. And I am completely rambling on." She took a deep breath. "So you really don't like Dallas?"

"My parents are here," he said. "And they aren't awesome."

She nodded, thinking better of pressing him for details. "That's a shame, about your parents and the bad taste rubbing off on Dallas. It's home for me, and I love it."

"Couldn't home be anywhere? Maybe not Austin, but New York, Chicago. Los Angeles."

She frowned, trying to seriously consider the question. Because the truth was, she'd had job offers from firms in all of those towns, each offering significantly more money than she was going to be making when she went into private practice in July. But she'd turned them all down. "When a place is home, you just know." She glanced sideways at him, caught his expression and grinned. "Or maybe you don't. Isn't Los Angeles home for you?"

He shook his head. "Like George Carlin said, it's a place for my stuff."

"Really?" The thought made her incredibly sad. "But you have a house out there, right?"

He nodded. "I'll probably be selling it, actually. No point in hanging on to it if I'm not going to be there."

"Where will you be?" She already knew he wasn't going to be here, in Dallas, with her.

"Overseas," he said, and the excitement in his voice was unmistakeable.

"Wanderlust?" Alyssa's boyfriend, Chris, was a travel writer, and Alyssa was currently in the process of rearranging her life to make it easier to travel with him. For Alyssa, that was great. Not so for Claire. She'd traveled enough as a child with her parents before high school finally grounded her. Now, she wanted to be settled. She wanted to slide into a community and really feel as if she was part of it. So far, she thought, she was off to a good start.

"Not so much wanderlust as chasing opportunity," he said. "I've had a dream for a while to open international locations of my clubs. Same name, exotic locations."

"And you're starting in Dallas?"

He laughed. "Kind of. My very first club was called Heaven, and I'm getting ready to launch the Dallas location in about a month."

"That's the one Joe wants to help you with."

"Right."

"Not to be obvious, but why did you pick Dallas?"

"I didn't. I pitched my plan to an investor, who liked the idea, but wanted me to prove myself. He owns Decadent, which was in the red when I arrived, and is now firmly in the black. And he did own the location where we're putting Heaven, though we're co-owners now. I pull that one off and show a solid revenue stream the first month, and he's willing to throw his weight behind me on the international front."

"That's so exciting."

"Yeah," he said. "I think so."

The GPS beeped to signal their arrival on her street, and she looked out with pride at the manicured lawn she'd taken such care with. The inside of the house still needed work, but she'd wanted curb appeal right off the bat. She and her friends had spent an entire Saturday prepping the house for painting, and then she'd spent the next five weekends plotting out a landscape design and then following up with all the planting. Now, in January, it was less impressive than it had been in the summer, but the house still looked charming and cheery, especially with the white Christmas lights twinkling against the blue trim.

"You'll have to excuse the mess inside," she said, leading him up the porch. "I'm doing the house in stages, and the first stage is the great room. So there's no floor at the moment, just a concrete slab. I'm trying to decide between hardwood, laminate or tile."

"You could stain the concrete," he said. "We did that at Heaven, and it looks great."

"Really? I hadn't thought of that." She'd thought stained concrete had to be done when the house was built, not after the fact, and she made a mental note to search the subject on Google.

"I could give you a hand," he said, the words making her hand pause on the way to putting the key in the lock and tilt her head up to look at him. His expression was perfectly bland, as if he didn't realize the import of what he'd said. And maybe he didn't. But to her, it was huge. To her, he'd just *de facto* told her that she was more than a one-night stand. And damned if that wasn't as much of a turn-on as anything else he'd said or done that evening.

"Thanks," she said, turning back to the key. "I'd like that a lot."

She led him in, then locked the door behind them, and when they were standing on her concrete floor with her garage-sale furniture that she'd replace after the room was complete, awkwardness started up again. He was in her home. He was going to help her with her floors. How had she gone from dateless and miserable to having this amazing man by her side? Had she won the sexual lottery and no one had bothered to tell her?

"So here we are," she said, dropping her tiny purse on the table.

"We are," he repeated, stepping close to her and making perfectly clear that whatever had sparked between them was still fizzling and popping.

Her body tingled, and her stomach tightened. Only not from desire, she realized. From hunger.

She slid her hand into his. "So, I know I promised you a specific kind of meal to follow the lovely appetizer we had in the break room, but now I'm wondering if I can tempt you with another kind of delicacy. The kind you actually eat."

He looked her up and down. "Oh, there was definitely eating on the agenda." His brows lifted as if he'd just figured something out. "Or did you mean food. Nutritional substances."

She bit back a smile. "For what you have in

mind, I think we both need fuel. Why don't we see what I've got?"

Not much, as it turned out, as she hadn't been to the grocery store in ages. Some Ritz crackers and peanut butter. Some white wine. Apples. Strawberries. A mostly empty container of vanilla ice cream. And a bottle of chocolate sauce. A few other odds and ends, but nothing that made up a meal, that was for sure.

She sighed. "There's probably something in the freezer or the pantry I can whip up," she said. "Take-out would take too long."

"Actually," he said, "is there anyplace that will deliver pizza this late?"

"Yup." The local pizza place had made it a point of leaving flyers on everyone's door announcing their intention to stay open until four on New Year's Eve, and of hiring extra drivers to cover the inevitable pizza emergencies.

"Why don't you order us whatever you want? In the meantime, I'll whip together a more traditional appetizer."

She shot a glance at the near-empty refrigerator, wondering if he had superhuman powers of food regeneration, then moved back to the hallway for her phone. When she returned, she found him washing strawberries, a bowl of chocolate with a spoon already on the counter.

"I microwaved it. You might want to make sure it's warm enough."

She drew the tip of her finger along the edge of the bowl, keeping her eyes on his, delighted to see the sparks fire when she brought the digit to her mouth and suckled. "Perfect," she said.

"Yes," he agreed. "Here." He dipped a strawberry, then brought it to her lips. She bit down, sending a dribble of chocolate spilling down her chin. She scooted backward, not wanting to get it on her dress, and he reached to steady her.

"Hang on," he said, moving in close and, apparently, pushing all of the air in the room out in the process. Because suddenly, she really couldn't breath. Especially not when he moved in even closer. When he drew his finger over her lip and offered the chocolate-tipped digit to her. And when she drew it in and sucked, oh, dear Lord, she was hot and wet and wondering how he could do that to her, so fast and so often.

"Missed a spot," he said, then slid his tongue over her lip. "Delicious. But you're right," he whispered, his hands reaching up to untie the halter of her dress. "This is too pretty to get covered with chocolate." Before she could protest—before she even realized what he was doing—he'd found the zipper on the skirt, as well. One flick down and the dress tumbled off her to pool around her ankles, leaving her standing naked in her kitchen, a fully clothed man in front of her with a very definitive gleam in his eye. "Beautiful," he said.

"Why do I have the feeling I'm the appetizer?" she asked.

He chuckled. "Clever girl. Come here." He tugged her toward him, then bent down and moved her dress out of the way. Then he dipped another strawberry, bringing it close to her, then teasing by pulling it away.

"Now you're being mean."

"Never."

A drop of chocolate flicked off, landing on the curve of her breast. She met his eyes, saw the intention there, and gasped as heat and pleasure coursed through her even before he closed his mouth to her skin. And when his tongue flicked over the chocolate—*oh, sweet succulent strawberries*—it was all she could do to keep from sliding her hand down between her legs and making herself come once again, this time in his arms.

"Let's try that again," he said, this time managing to get the strawberry to her mouth, but leaving her

lips surrounded by chocolate which he very purposefully and slowly licked off. Somehow, throughout it all, her knees continued to support. That was,
she thought, a miracle.

"Oops," he said, as another bit dribbled down,
this time into her cleavage. He licked it off, and she
almost screamed with the pleasure of it.

She reached for a strawberry herself, dipped it in
chocolate, and brought it to her mouth.

"No fair," he said. "I'm supposed to be feeding
you."

"Probably should," she said, trying very hard not
to grin. "I'm making such a mess." She dabbed the
strawberry to her chin, then closed her eyes as he
leaned in and licked it off.

"I see the problem," he said in a voice that promised so much.

She tried again, this time managing to miss her
mouth by at least a foot, the chocolate brushing
over her nipple instead. "Wow. I'm really a klutz."

"Happy to help you out," he said, then closed his
mouth and suckled, sending electric heat coursing
through her to pool between her thighs, burning and
throbbing with desperate need. So desperate that she
took another strawberry, then traced it down her
middle, over her bellybutton, then down, down, down.

"Oh, sweetheart," he said, then lowered himself to his knees, his hands at her waist holding her steady, his tongue flicking over her belly, setting her body on fire until she was nothing more than a giant ball of sexual heat and need.

Lower and lower he went, his tongue leading the way, dipping down, laving her skin clean and coming closer—so much closer—to where she wanted to feel him, the press of his lips upon her, his tongue caressing her, taking her higher and higher and—

*He was there,* and she gasped from the sensation, the feel of his mouth upon her so much more enticing than her fantasy could ever be. She curled her fingers in his hair silently urging him not to stop. She was close, her body already primed, and he played her with sweet intensity, taking her to the brink, then pulling back until she really and truly thought that she would go crazy. And then—right as the doorbell sounded to announce the arrival of pizza—he found her sweet spot and the world—and Claire—exploded.

# 5

"HERMIONE!" Claire called as her fuzzy orange cat batted playfully at Ty's earlobe. "Leave him alone."

She looked utterly sexy in baggy shorts and a T-shirt, and they were on the couch now, eating pizza out of the box, as Ty scrolled through the onscreen television guide. Claire had wanted control of the remote, but he'd jumped for it, determined not to have her landing on E! or TMZ or one of the other entertainment news channels that might be running some file footage of him. Or, God forbid, of her.

He tamped the thought down, realizing for the first time that there was a very real possibility that someone had posted a few pictures of the two of them together. He'd been less in the spotlight since coming to Dallas, but his picture still showed up at least five or six times each week, snapped by someone in the club eager to earn a fast buck selling to the networks and papers.

He really hoped everyone had been too busy celebrating their own New Year's to bother with him and Claire. Unlike most of the women he saw, he was certain Claire wouldn't be keen on being in the limelight.

Hopefully, he hadn't just firmly shoved her into it.

Behind him, Hermione sniffed at the pizza, then stepped tentatively on his shoulder as she headed toward the box.

"She's a smart thing," Claire said. "Very inquisitive."

"Thus the name," he said.

"Absolutely." She leaned across Ty's chest to scratch the cat behind the ears, and he breathed deep of her scent, now heavy on the chocolate and strawberries. "She's a rescue cat. I found her at the shelter. Poor thing was scheduled for the thing of which we do not speak." She pressed her finger to her lips. "Not in front of the cat, anyway."

He laughed. "Right." He pulled a glop of cheese off his pizza and held it up for the cat.

"Now you've done it," she said. "A friend for life."

"Not too bad," he said. "I can always use more furry orange friends."

"Can't we all."

She snuggled up against him, and he hooked

his arm around her shoulder, stopping the television on an old Bogart movie, then muting the sound so that they were watching Bogie and Bacall in silence, the tension between the two obvious even without sound.

"You can tell they were together in real life," Claire said. "It's that zing. You don't even need to hear them talk to know it's there. Bang and pop," she said, and then blushed.

"What's that?"

"Nothing. Just…chemistry."

"Right," he said, feeling at the moment as overwhelmed by chemistry as he had in high school when all the symbols and numbers for the various elements had flipped and turned and basically did a war dance just for his benefit. That had been the bad kind of overwhelmed. But this…

Well, who knew chemistry could be such a damn good thing?

Beside him, Claire yawned, and he realized that it was pushing 4:00 a.m. He was often up at that hour, working with the staff after closing, but he doubted that Claire was. "You look tired," he whispered, noting the way her eyes were drooping, as if it was all she could do not to succumb to sleep.

"Just what every girl wants to hear."

"You look tired," he repeated. "And beautiful."

She smiled at that. "I am," she admitted. "Tired, that is."

He stood and carried the pizza box to her kitchen, easily finding room for it in her fridge. "So tomorrow we're going to the party? Do we know what time or where?"

She reached out and tapped her phone on the coffee table, then tucked a pillow under her head and leaned it against the arm rest. "Checked it when the pizza arrived. Got a text from Joe. One o'clock. The Starr Resort."

"Nice," he said.

"I'm really sorry," she said, her voice thick with sleep. "I'm fading here." She licked her lips, her eyes catching his. "Do you want to stay the night?"

*Hell yes.* "I can't go like this tomorrow."

"Oh. Right. Well, that's okay. If you—"

"No, no," he rushed to clarify, the disappointment on her face about doing him in. "I just meant we'll have to swing by my place tomorrow so I can change. If that's okay."

"Of course." Her sleepy smile lit up her face. "That's no problem at all."

"Good," he said, going to her. "Great." With any luck, none of his roommates would be up. He hardly wanted to walk Claire into his personal version of *Animal House*.

He pressed a kiss to her forehead, then slid his arms underneath her, a soft, protective feeling gripping him as she curled up close. "I'm feeling like our score card is uneven," she said. "I'm two Big O's ahead of you."

He chuckled. "Trust me. That's one debt I'm going to collect." He was tempted to even the score right then. But she needed sleep, and the truth was, so did he.

She was already dozing by the time he pushed back her covers and slid her between the sheets, and watching her drove home how tired he was, too. He might be used to late nights, but he'd been cutting his sleep schedule short to get ready for the New Year's parties across his various establishments, and the lack of it was catching up to him.

He moved to the opposite side of the bed and climbed in, leaving his shoes and jeans on a chair nearby. He got settled on the pillow, then felt the heat of a warm steady glow when she rolled over and curled up against him. It wasn't anything real, he knew. Nothing serious. Only sleep. But there was something soft and sweet and gently wonderful about the press of the woman against him as the night hung heavy around them. He tried to remember the last time he'd truly wanted a woman in his bed— for sleeping that is—and no time sprang to mind.

With Claire, though…well, he wished it was *his* bed. And for the first time in the last six months, he regretted moving in with his buddy Matt. He could afford a place of his own a dozen times over, so why hadn't he rented a house? Or bought one, then kept it as an investment?

He knew the answer, of course. Mortgages and rental contracts were a little too much like moving back home, and that was something he wasn't going to do. Not with his parents just down the road in Plano. Not with their constant mantra in his ear that he'd never been quite good enough, that he needed to think about construction, that he'd be lucky to find a decent job. Even now, when he could point to his Malibu house and his bankroll and five pieces of prime Los Angeles real estate with a steady income stream—even now it didn't seem to be enough. Never once had his dad said he was proud of him. And the only time his mother ever called was to tell him that she saw him on TMZ, and what the devil was he doing getting himself noticed by such tripe?

It was all he could do to not ask her what she was doing watching it.

He loved them. He did. But he was tired of being a constant disappointment. Under the circumstances, he really wasn't sure what else he could do to win their approval. Better to live far away, out of the chill zone. As it was, they'd never once called to arrange breakfast or lunch or even a weekend gathering. He was right there in their town, and he might as well be thousands of miles away.

Maybe from thousands of miles away the sting would be less.

*No.* The sting already was less. He was used to it. His parents were who they were, and he dealt with that.

But that didn't mean he had to like it.

TY WOKE TO THE enticing feel of a woman's tongue flicking over his ear.

"Good morning," she whispered.

"What time is it?"

"Daytime," she said, and apparently that was all the information he was getting, because now she was trailing kisses down his neck and his arm, her fingers going to work on the tiny buttons of his shirt. "About that scorecard," she said, and although he couldn't see her mouth, he could hear the smile in her voice, not to mention the heat, and his body, only moments before groggy with sleep, twitched to life.

She shifted her weight, lifting her head to smile at him. "Any complaints? Comments? Observations for the record?"

"I think I'd be wise to just let you handle this one."

"Good answer," she said, then lifted herself up and—oh, please give him strength now—straddled him right at his hips, her rear brushing his very hard, very awake cock. "No touching," she said. "Hands at your sides. This is all about me touching you."

She leaned forward, her lips brushing his jaw, her fingers sliding deep into his hair. "If I can make you feel even half as good as you made me last night, you're going to be one very happy man." Her mouth shifted left, then her teeth nipped at his earlobe, and Ty was certain that he was going to lose it right then. "Kiss me," she said, and then closed her mouth over his as if to prove how very serious she was about the demand.

Demanding and hungry and yet sweet at the same time, she took total charge of the kiss, exploring his mouth with her tongue, biting and nipping on his lips, taking and giving and teasing and making promises with her body that he couldn't wait for her to keep.

She broke the kiss with a teasing little nip to his

lower lip, then pressed a soft finger there. "Don't move," she said, then scooted down, down, until her hands cupped his briefs and the massive erection straining for release. She positioned herself over him, her panties against his briefs, her clit rubbing over his cock, and she kissed him, hard and deep, then slid kisses across his jaw until she got to his ear. "Do you like that?"

"God, yes."

"Can you feel how wet I am?"

He groaned, completely helpless to this woman who'd taken control of his body. "Claire." He ground her name out, like a prayer. Like a plea. "Let me touch you."

"Shh," she said, then nipped his chin. "You're not going to do anything. Just me. You know how to play by the rules, right?"

He could only nod, as all the blood that would normally operate the part of his brain that formed words had flowed downstream to his cock, which she released by gently easing the band of the briefs down until it sprang free, proud and begging for attention.

Her hand reached down to stroke him, and he felt the pressure build, that sweet climb toward release and heaven. He wanted it, and yet he didn't. He wanted this to last, and yet he wanted the explosion.

Hell, he just wanted.

Most of all, though, he wanted her. Wanted to be inside her again. Wanted to hear her come in his ear and know that he'd brought her there. That he'd taken her high and hard.

This was her game, though, and if that's the way she wanted it, he'd survive. And soon he'd render the same type of sweet torture on her.

Her nimble fingers stroked his shaft, the friction of palm against his flesh nearly bringing him to the edge.

And then, when he felt her tongue dance over the tip—then, he was certain that he really had died and gone to heaven.

She said his name once, then closed her mouth over him, the sweet, warm heat of her soft mouth stroking him even as her hands touched him in all the right spots. It was a sensual assault, and Ty was not a strong enough man to hold out. He'd been on the verge since he'd discovered the taste of chocolate mixed with Claire, and now he let the sensation build. Let the tension flow and collect. Let the pleasure grow, until he couldn't stand it anymore and the entire universe exploded around him, leaving only him and Claire and the sense that he'd just experienced one absolutely perfect moment.

She shifted, then eased herself back up his sensitive body, curling herself up beside him and hooking a leg over his hip. Her calf brushed his cock, which twitched, possibly in thank you, possibly in regret that round two wasn't immediately on the agenda.

"Good morning," she whispered. "I hope you liked your wake-up call."

WITH HER HAIR DAMP and her fluffy robe wrapped tight around her, Claire scrolled through her text and phone messages while Ty showered. She'd considered taking him up on his suggestion that they save water and shower together, but they'd slept incredibly late and according to Joe's text message, the party was only from one to three, and already it was past eleven.

They needed to get dressed and out the door soon, because they still had to get to Ty's, get him a change of clothes, and then get all the way to far north Dallas by no later than one-thirty. Fashionably late was one thing, but any time after that would be downright rude.

If they hurried, they'd make it, but as they'd already discovered, *hurry* was not a word that applied when the two of them were naked. Get in the shower together, it might be another full year before they made it to the Power Publicity party.

She had a huge number of e-mails from friends

probably wishing her "Happy New Year," that she vowed to read later, and then one text from Alyssa labeled *Have U Seen Ths?*

Since she had absolutely no idea what that could be referring to, she opened the message and found herself staring right back at herself. And not just her. Her and Ty, locked in a clench, their pose definitely suggesting that they were going to find a private place and do exactly what they did.

*Oh, shit.*

She scrolled the message down and found Alyssa's included note:

Showed up on Twitter. Not sure who found it first, but wanted U to see. He's amazing, but....

Claire drew in a breath, thinking about where that picture had been. Some Web site. Then some blogs. Then Twitter. Good Lord, all of her friends would have seen it. Not that she was ashamed or anything. After all, if they'd been at the club they would have seen the same thing, right? But still…

She kept scrolling and found another message, this one labeled, *Be Careful.*

She clicked it open with dread, and found a full article which included the picture. An article all about Ty, and how he always had a different woman on his arm, and oh-lookey-here, the next one is Claire Daniels, a Dallas attorney and daughter of Senator Anthony Daniels. Good Lord, she thought, as something cold and unwelcoming eased up her spine. She was gossip. How the hell had that happened? More, what the hell did she intend to do about it?

Not a question she had time to ponder, because now Ty was coming back into the room, a towel hooked around his waist, his body damp and delicious and good enough to eat. His eyes found Claire's and her body went all hot and fizzy, like he'd flipped some sort of switch on her. And, damn her, she couldn't deny that she liked the way it felt.

Ty took one look at her and frowned. "Are you okay? You're not dressed."

She closed her hand around the phone in her pocket. "Fine. Just hungover."

"Aspirin," he said, then started rummaging in her medicine cabinet. And as Claire watched him tap out a couple of pills, she sighed, wishing that Aspirin really did have the power to cure what ailed her.

# 6

"YOU LIVE HERE? It's huge."

Ty pulled into the long driveway, bringing the car to a halt in front of the sprawling stone home. "Temporarily," he said. "And it's a friend's. He travels a lot. Thought it would be a good idea to have someone else share the mortgage."

He came around to open her door, then took her arm as they walked up the path. She didn't pull away, but he neither did she look at him the way she'd looked at him the night before. In fact, he had the distinct impression that she was afraid to look at him, as if she'd give away something she didn't want revealed.

He wanted to push her on it and make her tell him what was bothering her, but he knew he didn't have the right. There was no relationship between them. No commitment. But if she was having regrets about last night, he damn sure hoped she got over it. For his part, he had no regrets at all. For the first time in a long time, in fact, he wanted to stay with the woman he'd slept with. And not just in bed. Already he was cursing the damn party, because he wanted to take her out to breakfast, show her the funky local places he'd found.

He just plain wanted to spend time with her, and that was not a feeling that tended to be high up there on Ty Coleman's list of emotional states. He couldn't even remember the last time he'd been in a serious relationship. Lately, women had been dates. Distractions. Booty-call buddies.

He didn't fully understand why, but there was no denying that Claire was more than that. Which was why her sudden slide into pensiveness made him so uncomfortable.

"I won't take long," he said, leading her into the house, only to find it a hell of a lot more hectic than he'd left it.

He'd forgotten about football, of course, and now at least two dozen guys were sprawled out in the massive living room, screaming at the television set.

Claire turned to him, her amused expression lightening his own mood a thousand-fold. "All of them live here?"

"Only a small percentage," Ty said.

"Ty!" one of the guys yelled. "These douchebags are playing for shit! You outta just buy the team. Fire that lousy-ass coach."

"Yeah, buy the team!"

"Hell, just buy more beer!"

After that, he couldn't hear as his former frat brothers, current roommates, and a few assorted strangers all started shouting things at once. From the far side of the room, Matt stood up and motioned to the kitchen. Ty pressed his hand to Claire's back and steered them that direction.

"I'm Matt," Ty's friend and current landlord said, holding out his hand for Claire. "Since I don't know you, I'm guessing you came with Ty and not for football."

"You guessed right." To her credit, she didn't seem overwhelmed, either by the crowd in the other room or by Matt, who fully qualified as a bear of a man, his huge paw managing to completely engulf her hand as he shook it.

"We're late," Ty said. "Just came in to get fresh clothes."

"Right. I'll follow you up." He turned to Claire. "I need to talk to my boy. Would you mind—"

"No, of course not," she said, then pulled out a chair at the table. "I'm happy to wait."

"Help yourself to anything in the fridge, if there's anything left. If it's not nailed down around here, it gets eaten pretty quickly."

Ty mouthed a quick, *sorry,* to which she replied with a definitive, *don't worry about it,* and then he followed Matt out of the room.

"What's up?" he asked, when they reached the room that Ty had been renting for the last six months. He started stripping down, happy to get into some clean clothes.

"Does she realize who you are?"

He turned, surprised. "Excuse me?"

"You need to check your phone more often, dude. Give it here." Ty passed Matt his phone, then slid on a clean shirt while Matt tapped at the touchscreen. "Check it out."

Ty took the phone and looked at the crystal clear screen. A screen showing, up close and personal, him and Claire tight in a clench. Exactly what he'd feared, and even faster than he'd expected.

"That explains it then," he said.

"What?"

"After I got out of the shower this morning. A chill in the air. She checked her messages. How much do you want to bet she's gotten a hundred e-mails with this picture."

"She's an attorney, Ty. Works for a judge."

"You know her?" Matt worked at one of the largest law firms in the city.

"Not personally, but I've heard of her. She's active in the Bar, attends a lot of fund-raisers. Just accepted a job at Thatcher and Dain in their appellate section, and that's a hard nut to crack, let me tell you."

"And her dad's a senator," Ty said. "Thanks for showing me."

"Dallas may be the big city, bro, but this town still turns on gossip. It may be more polite in the South than it is in California, but it cuts just as deep."

Ty ran his fingers through his hair, silently cursing.

"She one of your usuals, or one you want to hang on to for a while?"

Ty buttoned his slacks as he looked toward the door, imagining Claire at the kitchen table, scrolling through e-mails asking her who the devil she'd gotten mixed up with.

For a moment, Ty considered denying how he felt, but this was Matt, his best friend. The guy who'd had his back when Ty had been dumb enough to put firecrackers in Old Lady Beckett's mailbox, and had walked the walk of shame with him when guilt had settled in his gut and he'd gone to confess his crime.

They knew each other's secrets, and although Ty

didn't share everything with his friends, with Matt, he shared a lot. "I like her, Matt. I really like her."

His friend's shoulders sagged, ever so slightly. "Okay, then. I'll keep a good thought for you, guy. But I wouldn't be surprised if for the first time in a long time, you're the one standing still, and the girl's the one doing the walking away."

"I'M SO SORRY ABOUT the picture," Ty said when they were back in the car and heading north on the tollroad.

"You saw?"

"Matt showed me." He sighed, gripping the steering wheel tighter. "I expect that kind of thing when I'm in L.A., but I didn't think to warn you. I'm sorry about that."

"It's okay," she smiled, and right then he really believed that it *was* okay, and his heart leaped a little, knowing that he hadn't inadvertently ruined everything for her—or kicked her out of his life.

"It's not your fault," she added.

He nodded in agreement, though he supposed to be technical, he could argue that point. After all, he'd cultivated the lifestyle. He'd courted the tabloids and the paparazzi. He'd done everything he could to get his name out there as much as possible and as often as possible.

He'd wouldn't do it any differently now, because in the market he worked in, that was what it took to build interest. But that didn't change the basic fact that he retained some level of responsibility for Claire ending up on the Internet in a clench.

"It was just one kiss," she said, philosophically. "It's not as if they got pictures of anything else." He glanced sideways and noted her small frown. "Did they?"

"I checked. Nothing. I think we're clear."

"Well, there you go. New Year's Eve. One kiss. It's silly."

She reached over and stroked his hand, and the simple touch caused a wave of pleasure to flow through him. Intensely sensual, but also, well, *nice.* A sensation he now associated only with Claire.

"I've sorry if I seemed moody earlier," she said. "This is new territory for me."

"And you don't like it."

The corner of her mouth curved up in a wry grin. "Not much. No."

And that, he thought, was something else that set her apart from other girls. Instead of chasing celebrity, Claire was content to calmly step out of its raging path.

"If I'm going to be noticed," she said, "I want it

to be for something other than the quality of my kiss or the gorgeousness of the man I'm kissing."

"I'm not sure if that's a compliment, but I'll take it as one."

"It is," she said, her voice lightened by her smile. "And I'm fine now. Really."

SHE MEANT IT, too, but even if she hadn't, she probably would have said so anyway, especially now that she saw how concerned he'd been that she'd bolt and run. And, yeah, she'd considered bolting and running. But it was one picture. One silly little New Year's Eve picture that made the rounds among her friends and would soon be forgotten.

After all, it wasn't as if *she* was a celebrity. No news story there.

And it wasn't as if she'd be kissing Ty in public everyday, though private was a different matter altogether. And, yes, she hoped to be full up on private kisses, and other indoor sports, as well.

Honestly, she'd completely overreacted, and so had Alyssa. Time for them both to chill.

He turned down the Starr Resort's private driveway, then navigated over the grounds. The property was part Resort, and part working ranch, with small cabins dotted over the property that people could rent out for the weekend, as well as a five-star hotel.

Today, their destination was the hotel, and Ty took them down into the underground parking labyrinth. They took the elevator up to the lobby level, Claire's body thrumming simply from the way Ty was holding her hand, his thumb idly grazing her skin. When the doors opened, she gasped, and this time it had nothing to do with the man beside her, but instead by the magnificence of the room.

She'd been to a lot of fancy hotels and conference halls, but this one was by far the most impressive. A giant Christmas tree dominated the room, the far side of which was made entirely of windows that opened out onto the fabulous patio with stone tables, water falls and a view of the cows wandering in the field behind.

The room itself was cavernous, but nothing seemed to get lost, and as Claire stood taking it all in, pondering the possibility of a similarly distressed wood floor for her living room, a bellman appeared beside them to ask if they needed help.

"Power Publicity," Ty said, and they were immediately shown the way to a spectacular ballroom in which the PR firm had clearly invested approximately the gross national product of a small country. Two of the four walls were lined with food stations, the other two with bars. In case you didn't want to wait, waiters circulated with trays of popular drinks and appetizers. And dotted throughout the room were six blackjack stations. Each guest, they were told by a helpful young woman wearing a Power Publicity pin announcing her name as Anna, received five hundred "dollars" in chips. At the end of the night, they could cash in their winnings for a various bits of swag donated by clients of Power, or they could donate the chips themselves, and Power would make an equivalent donation to a local charity.

It was, thought Claire, a brilliant setup, and since she was currently working with a charitable committee, she made a quick note to investigate acquiring chips and blackjack tables.

"Roulette's good, too," Ty said, peering at the note. "But what do you want them for?"

"I'm on the fund-raising committee for a local literacy organization. Our big event is coming up, so…" She caught his expression. "What?"

"Nothing. Just…literacy. It's a good cause. I'm impressed."

She lifted a brow. "Thanks. It's important to me. Are you sure you're okay?"

He nodded toward the far side of the room. "There's Joe and Bonita. Shall we go take care of the social niceties?"

"And do a little business," she said. "Didn't you want to talk to him about PR?"

"Social niceties are the heart of business," he said, taking her arm. "I learned that one a long time ago."

"You came!" Bonita said, as they approached. "I'm so glad. Now, you two be sure to get a drink, and don't you even hesitate to eat. We have so much food, I swear, we should invite the Dallas Cowboys."

"Next year," Joe said. "I'm working on landing that account."

Bonita leaned over and kissed his temple, and Claire thought that he flinched, just a little. "I'm going to go circulate. I know Daddy's around here somewhere. You take care of our guests," she said to Joe, pointing at Claire and Ty.

"I've got it under control," he said. He nodded toward her. "Claire. You look wonderful. Nice picture, too." He caught Ty's eye. "For you, I think you hit the right note. But, Claire, darling, considering your profession, you should try to avoid raising your EQ."

"EQ?"

"Your entertainment quotient. Publicity—that's okay. So long as it's the right kind. If you're going to present yourself to the public, you have to be sure it's the right image you're putting forward."

"Yes, well, had I been the one putting that image forward, I'm sure I would have considered those factors." She sounded snippy to her own ears, but she'd almost managed to put the picture out of her mind, and wasn't thrilled to have it brought back up to the forefront. "I'm going to leave you two to talk," she said, figuring an exit was her best plan of attack at the moment. "I think I saw a few people I know over by the bar."

She took a step away, and was stopped by a single word from Ty. "Claire." Her name seemed to reverberate through her, his voice full of decadent promises. She turned back to him, her brow rising in question. "Soon," he said, and all she could do was swallow and try not to let her head fill with images of exactly what "soon" would entail.

Gathering herself, she headed back into the throng. She'd seen at least a dozen familiar faces when they'd arrived, and now she intended to circulate, network and make great contacts. For the most part, her plan went pretty well. In less than twenty minutes, she'd chatted with two retired judges now in private practice, one of whom also knew and respected Judge Monroe. But when it became apparent that he intended to dominate her time, she made an excuse, then headed over to one of the buffets to check out the selection of truly tempting desserts and appetizers.

A hand grazed her back, the touch already so familiar she didn't even have to turn around. "Hungry?"

"Starved," he said, though from his tone, she really didn't think he was talking about food.

She laughed. "I'd feed you, but I don't want to end up in the papers." She pressed her plate into his hand. "Here. Help yourself."

"It's a sad lot when all a woman will give me is her plate of food."

"Yes, I can see how you've had it rough lately."

"I could go for a little bit rough," he said, taking a step closer so that the air between them sizzled. "You?"

"Ty…" She shifted, her body tingling, images she really didn't need to have in her head right then filling her mind. Him ripping off her panties. Slamming her back against a wall. Pounding inside of her.

"You're blushing."

"Stop it…"

He lowered his voice, pitching it only for her. "You're thinking about later. What I'll do to you. What we'll do together."

"No, I—"

"Liar."

His tease rolled over her, as light as butterfly wings. "All right. I am."

"Me, too. Want me to tell you what we're going to do?"

*Say no. Tell him to circulate. Get yourself together.* "Yes."

"Parchesi."

"Par—*what?*" She looked into his eyes, certain he was joking, but there was nothing but heat there. Heat, and a, yeah, tiny spark of amusement.

"Fabulous game," he said, taking a step toward her. "Very engaging."

She swallowed. "Is that a fact?"

"Of course, if you don't like Parchesi…"

"I don't know how to play," she said, as a thin man scooted in toward the buffet and started piling shrimp on a plate. She shifted to give him more room, the motion taking her closer to Ty. She breathed him in, like soap and mint. She wanted to touch him, but she held back, the simple act of denial making her more needy. "Will you teach me?"

"I think we can arrange a few lessons," he said,

ignoring the man with the shrimp, his eyes only on her. "Are you a fast learner?"

"Terribly slow," she said, and saw the corner of his mouth twitch with a suppressed smile. "You may have to show me over and over and over again before I figure it out."

"Don't worry," he said. "I can be patient. Very patient."

"I'm so glad to hear it."

"Maybe we can—"

"Claire?" The male voice came from behind, and she turned to find herself looking into the face of one of her law-school study buddies, Hunter.

"Look at you!" she cried, giving him a quick hug, then introducing him to Ty. "How are you? What are you up to these days?"

Ty, who apparently didn't care for attorney banter, stayed only long enough to be polite, then told her they'd finish discussing the game later before off into the crowd again.

"Game?"

"Football."

"Aren't you the one who hated football?"

"It's not up there on my top ten," she said, then steered the conversation back to the much more safe topic of him. "Last I heard you were working in Washington."

"Did that. Moved back here to spearhead a first amendment practice area. I hear you're leaving the cushy government world for the hard-edged practice of appellate law soon."

She laughed. "Rumors travel fast in this town."

She thought his eyes shifted toward Ty, but she couldn't be sure. "Yes," he said. "They do. Anyway, when I saw you, I wanted to touch base. I'm always interested in working with the appellate team at the beginning of a case. Makes for a cleaner record that way."

"Maybe we should arrange a meeting after I'm settled," she said, and as they were exchanging business cards Mellie Jo Patterson came up beside them and gave Hunter a kiss. "Look at you two," she said. "My fiancé and my committee co-chair already old friends."

"We've been friends for a while," Claire said. "Hunt and I went to law school together."

"No way. Small world."

"And getting smaller," Hunt said. "Claire's the one you're chairing the literacy fund-raiser with?" he asked MJ.

"Guilty," Claire said.

He pressed a kiss to MJ's temple. "In that case, I'll let you two talk." He caught Claire's eye. "Make sure she invites you over for dinner sometime. It would be nice to catch up. And to discuss the law with someone who knows what a penumbra is."

MJ rolled her eyes. "I thought it was a brand of stoneware," she said. "Only once. And I'll never live it down. At any rate, I wanted to talk to you about your new guy."

A little burst of dread shot through Claire. "Excuse me?"

"That's him, right?" she asked, pointing across the room to where Ty was standing with a man talking animatedly with his hands. "I saw the thing going around on Twitter—"

"Gee. Great."

"—and I think this could be a real opportunity."

Claire waited, because so far she wasn't seeing the opportunity for anything more than annoyance.

"A celebrity auction!" MJ said, clapping her hands with so much enthusiasm Claire was surprised heads weren't turning in the room.

"I'm not really sure he's—"

"Not him, silly," MJ said. "I thought you could ask him to donate a friend of his." Her lips pursed together in thought. "Actually, though, we could do *Win a date with Ty*—"

"I'll talk to him," Claire said, because as much as the thought of auctioning Ty off to some other woman curled up her insides, she couldn't deny that it was a brilliant suggestion on MJ's part. And with Ty's involvement, they could expand their guest list to include celebrities with even the remotest Hollywood connections. With that kind of starpower, they could probably bring in triple the donations over last year. And anything that could accomplish that was definitely worthwhile.

She caught a glimpse of Bonita moving swiftly through the room toward the patio doors, her head down, ensuring she made eye contact with nobody. She looked so distressed, that Claire's heart twisted a little. "I'll ask him and be in touch," Claire said to MJ. "But listen, will you excuse me? I need to go see about something."

She wove through the crowd, then slipped out of the room the same way Bonita had. She found the other woman sitting under a gazebo, blowing her nose on a tissue. She looked up as Claire approached, her eyes red and swollen.

"Bonita? What's wrong?"

"Joe," Bonita said, practically spitting the word. "I saw him. I freaking *saw him.*"

"Saw him doing what?" Claire asked, warning bells flashing bright in her mind.

"With *her*. His hand was up her skirt and he was practically sucking her face off. Oh, God, oh, God." She looked up at Claire with puffy, damp eyes. "Men are pigs."

Claire felt ice cold. "You're sure? You couldn't be mistaken?"

Bonita dug her smartphone out of her purse, punched a button and passed it to Claire. "Least I was thinking clear, huh? I wanted evidence in case he tried to deny being a filthy, cheating pig." She snuffled. "Did he ever do that to you? Cheat?"

"I— No. Not that I know of, anyway."

"Well, that's the real trick, isn't it. I wouldn't have even found out if I hadn't stumbled into the wrong room, looking for the bathroom. *They were in a storage closet!* I mean, how tacky is that? *Bastard.*"

"How long have you two been dating?"

Bonita nibbled on her thumb, thinking. "Two months. Closer to three, actually."

Claire swallowed. She didn't know if Joe had cheated *on* her, but she knew now that he'd tried to cheat on Bonita *with* her. She weighed the benefit of telling the girl and decided it would only hurt her more. "What are you going to do?"

"Dump his ass, what do you think? Like I'd stay with a womanizing scum." She drew in a long, slow breath. "But it still hurts, you know?"

"I know." She hooked an arm around the other woman's shoulder. "Do you think you can go back inside? Do you want me to get anything for you?"

"Got a giant club I can whack the bastard in the face with?"

"Probably best to lay off the whacking until you cool down."

"Yeah," Bonita said, standing up and smoothing her skirt. "You're right." She pointed around the side of the building. "I'm going to go in that way and clean myself up."

"Do you want me to come with you?"

She shook her head. "You're supersweet, but I'll be okay." She started to walk away, then stopped and looked back. "And, Claire? Thanks."

They parted, and Claire headed back into the party, her mind filled with thoughts of Joe and cheating and womanizing men-pigs. It made for quite a messy rush of noise in her mind, which probably explained how she almost walked straight into Malcolm Thatcher, her new boss-to-be.

"Oh! Mr. Thatcher. So good to see you here."

"Claire, what a lovely surprise. And fortuitous.

I was meaning to call you. We're all so very excited that you're joining the firm soon, but in the meantime, I was wondering if I could steal an hour or so of your time one day—if the Judge doesn't mind—to have you come into the office."

"Of course," she said, trying not to let her confusion show. "I'd be happy to. Can I ask why?"

He waved away the question as if it were nothing, but Claire had the distinct impression he was being purposefully vague. "Nothing major. Just office policy. Housekeeping. That kind of thing."

"Sure. I'll talk to Judge Monroe and let you know what day would be the most convenient."

"Perfect," he said. "Now you go enjoy the party. Jake Powers certainly knows how to throw them."

He certainly did. The party was jam-packed with so many people that she wanted to meet, either professionally or to discuss the charity auction, that by the time she'd made it across the room to Ty, she'd all but forgotten the odd conversation with Malcolm Thatcher.

He was talking to a guy who held himself so straight he seemed prissy, and from Ty's overly polite expression, Claire had the distinct impression that the man had been droning on and on endlessly about his company's commercial alarm systems.

Considering the snippet of conversation she overheard, she felt no guilt about stepping up to rescue Ty. "Hi," she said, thrusting her hand out for the company man to shake. "I'm Claire, and I'm so sorry to have to steal him away, but we have a small Parchesi emergency."

"I— Oh." He blinked, clearly confused. "Well, an emergency. Of course."

And they left him standing there, completely befuddled.

"Thank you," Ty said. "I'm pretty sure my ears were going to fall off. And if your emergency involves heading back to your house and rolling around in the sheets naked, I'd like to say that I'm now a big believer in the power of visualization."

"You've been visualizing naked sheet rolling?" she said.

"In color. With sound effects."

She laughed. "And the rating?"

"R for the dialogue and banter, NC-17 for the main event."

She lifted a brow. "Not X?"

"I like to keep an open mind," he said, twining his fingers with hers. "Maybe we should go all out, and if need be, we can always leave the X bits on the cutting-room floor."

"Now?"

"Hell yes. I've talked to Joe. I've talked to at least half a dozen attorneys who want to represent me and another half-dozen who want to take my organization public, and two music managers who think I should sign their up-and-coming bands to play my club circuit in L.A. I'm not sure who else is here that would be interested in talking to me. Which," Ty added with a significant look her way, "is a very good thing. Because I'm ready to get out of here. How about you?"

"Most definitely," she said, her body firing in anticipation. She tried to remember if any other man had been able to switch her motor on so easily. Just one look, and she was purring. Then again, she thought as she saw Bonita chatting in a corner, maybe Ty simply knew how to push a woman's buttons. After all, he'd had a lot of practice with a lot of women.

"Claire?" He frowned, looking at her. "Something wrong?"

She shook the ill thoughts away. Ty wasn't Joe. And her reaction to him wasn't tied to anything he said or did. Not connected to any silly flirting games he played. Instead it was all about the man. He'd gotten under her skin. And although that scared her a little, there was no denying it excited her, too.

"There are a few more people I could talk to," she admitted. "But…"

"What?"

She met his eyes. "The truth is I don't think I can stand even five more minutes without your hands on me."

A raw carnality seared his eyes, the intensity echoing her own desire. "Claire," he said, her name sounding like a prayer on his lips. "Come on."

They moved through the thinning crowd with purpose, then stopped in front of the elevator to the parking garage. The doors slid open, and they entered a blissfully empty elevator car. And when the door slid closed and started descending, he pulled her in close, pressing her body to his. "Thank God. I wasn't sure how much longer I could wait to get my hands on you."

Claire was pretty sure the heat they were generating had melted her bones, because she had no choice but to cling to him or else fall to the ground. She could feel him against her, hard and ready, and she knew it was because of her. *Her.*

The thought made her tremble. Made her wet.

His palms grazed her nipples, and she moaned, then silently cursed as the elevator dinged, and they broke apart as the doors slid open on the first parking level. Another couple stepped on, a respectable distance between them, one complaining to the other that he should have paid more attention to where he'd left the car.

Ty eased back, leaning against the wall behind her. The couple was in front of them, watching the door, and Claire almost jumped when she felt Ty's hand on the back of her thigh. Then sneaking up under the back of her dress. His fingers stroking, so soft and gentle, and she was getting wet, so very very wet. Already her panties were soaked, a fact he soon realized as his naughty fingers climbed higher, then slipped inside.

She squealed, the covered the sound with a cough when the man shifted quickly, turning to cast a glance at her.

She tried to smile casually, which was hard to do, as Ty's finger had found its way to her clit, and now he was stroking in long, wet strokes, the feeling of the building climax contrasting with the dangerous naughtiness of public elevator sex, the pleasure so intense that she was pretty sure she was going to have to have the coughing fit to beat all, simply so that she could disguise a raging, blinding orgasm.

The elevator stopped and the couple got off.

She twirled around, hitting the emergency stop button before pinning Ty against the wall, and taking the hand that had been teasing her so desperately and sliding it back inside her panties, shimmying a little as her body urged him on. No other man had ever made her feel like this. Wild and wanton and desperate for his touch. To be consumed. As if she wouldn't be satisfied until she was nothing more than a pile of blazing embers, burnt up by his touch.

"You cannot," she moaned, forcing the words out, "can*not* tease me like that and then not follow through."

"Anything you say," he said, his voice pure heat.

She was close, so damn close, and so incredibly turned on. When he bent his mouth to her breast and pushed the flimsy material aside to suckle on her taut, tender nipple, she really and truly thought she was going to lose it right then.

"Now. Please. Just *now.*" Her fingers were on his fly, and she was tugging his zipper down, then urging his pants down over his hips. His cock sprang free, completely comfortable with the *now* plan. He turned her around, pressing her hands up against the wall of the elevator, then flipping the back of her skirt up over her ass. He ripped her panties off, and she couldn't have cared less. Anything to get him inside her faster before she died simply from the need of him.

One hand cupped her breast and she heard him slip on a condom, then felt the tip of his cock rubbing against her sex, making them both slick and ready.

*"Now,"* she repeated, because she couldn't stand not having him again. Touching her. Inside her. Thrusting and moaning as she stretched around him, taking him in deeper and deeper as they moved in perfect unison.

He kept one hand on her breast and the other he slipped down to cup her crotch, the tip of his finger finding her clit. And as his cock ravaged her, his finger teased her, until she found herself crying out his name and floating through the air, the orgasm taking her to places she really hadn't gone before. As she went limp, he stiffened, his own orgasm sending a few more red-hot sparks of curling, swirling pleasure dancing through her.

They collapsed together, and only when they were still did they hear the voices that seemed to be surrounding them. They caught each other's eyes, both fighting not to laugh as Ty shoved her panties into his pocket and then stood up, holding out a hand to help her do the same.

"Somehow, you always get me out of my panties."

"It's one of my favorite pastimes," he retorted, then switched the elevator back to run as Claire smoothed her dress. The car cranked back to life, finally opening on their floor, where four people were gathered.

"This really is the world's slowest elevator," one of them commented.

Claire just shrugged, fighting a smile. "Really? It sure seemed fast to me."

# 7

THEY'D FOLLOWED UP mind-blowing elevator sex with sweet bedroom sex, and now Ty was leaning back against Claire's matching pillow shams, wondering what the hell he was going to do about this. Because she'd gotten under his skin in a big way. *A big way.* And right then the only thing he could think to do about it was enjoy the flow and see where they were in two months. Because as much as he wanted the hell out of Dallas, leaving the city meant leaving the woman, and that reality was barreling down on him like a huge express train that he was doing his best to ignore.

Ideally, he'd take her with him. Show her Paris. London. See the world.

And, yeah, he'd suggest it.

But he already knew her well enough to know that she'd turn him down. Women who matched their pillow shams to their curtains to the prints hanging on the walls didn't want to live out of a suitcase for nine months. That much, he accepted as a truism.

"You look lost," she said, coming back into the room with two glasses of wine. "And I feel very decadent. Hanging out in bed in the middle of the afternoon, drinking wine."

"I was lost in thoughts of you," he said, "and right now, there's no where I'd rather be than in bed." He shifted, taking the wine from her, then scooting over to make room. She sat close, the tank top she wore thin enough the he could see the outline of her nipples, and despite the fact that he'd just tasted that particular fruit, his body hardened again with need. *Down, boy.* This wasn't all about sex. Not with Claire. Not anymore.

Hell, maybe it never was. But the sex was damn sure a solid perk of whatever was growing between them.

"You still haven't told me how you fared. Did you charm every lawyer in the city?"

"Of course. How could I not?" She laughed, then took a sip of wine. "Seriously, it was good. I met a lot of people, got some great leads, and also MJ had a terrific idea for this charity function we're organizing for next month. Actually, I could use your help."

"Me? What do you need?"

"You, actually," she said with a wicked grin. "And maybe a friend."

He narrowed his eyes. "Spit it out."

"A bachelor auction. And if you could ask one of the actresses you know in L.A. to come out here for a 'Lunch With the Star' thing, we could let people bid and have a whole group. I know it's a lot to ask, but I really think it would bring in the money, and it's for a good cause."

"Literacy."

"Right."

"And I'd be the bachelor."

"Uh, yeah."

"Would you bid?"

"Of course," she said. "But if this works out the way we want, I'll be out of the running pretty early on. Government attorney here, remember? That means government salary."

"And it won't kill you to watch me auctioned off to another woman?" He'd been teasing, but from the shadow that crossed her face, he realized that it really would bug her. And knowing that brought a serious smile to his face. "Hey," he said. "I won't do it if you don't want me to."

"You read me too easily," she countered, then

drew in a breath. "I'm just selfish and don't want to share. But of course I want you to do it. The cause is important to me."

"Me, too. And since you want me to, I will."

"Thanks. So why is it important to you?" she asked. "I don't mean to pry, and don't feel like you have to tell me, but you looked...I don't know... *distant* when I first mentioned it at the party."

It wasn't something he talked about. It wasn't even something he liked thinking about. But it was part of him, part of who he was. And, yeah, he wanted to share it with her. "I'm dyslexic," he said. "Reading and numbers...absolute hell for me."

She shifted so that she was facing him, her expression both serious and compassionate. But not pitying, and for that he was grateful. "Were you diagnosed as a child? I was under the impression that if you're diagnosed young you could learn coping mechanisms so that reading isn't as much of a chore."

"Yes, well, I wasn't. And by the time I did have a school counselor who saw a kid with a learning disability instead of a cutup, well, by that time everyone, my parents included, had pegged me as subpar. Someone who better make sure he knew how to work the fryer at a fast-food joint, because that was going to be the best that kid could do."

As much as he tried to tell himself it didn't matter, he could still hear his parents telling him not to apply to college because they knew he wouldn't be accepted. They were more astounded than he was when he actually got in, but he'd become a self-fulfilling prophecy when he'd dropped out, his challenges with words and numbers making it far too difficult to keep up in classes.

Claire was holding his hand, and now she squeezed. "That's horrible. I'm so sorry your parents were so—"

"That's just who they are," he said. "I've accepted it. And I'm fine. I listen to a lot of audio books, rely on spellcheck on the computer like you wouldn't believe and hired an accountant my first day in Los Angeles. I'm doing fine."

"Yeah," she said, "you are." She leaned over and pressed a soft kiss on his cheek. "I think you're amazing. And I think that what you've told me makes you even more perfect for our bachelor auction. Can we use your story? Not the bit about your parents, but just the challenges?"

He considered the question, because the truth wasn't something that he particularly wanted broadcast. He'd lived his life in the public eye, but that was a facade, not the real Ty. But at the same time...

"Do you think it matters?"

"Are you kidding? Look at what you've accomplished. You're a role model. And the fact that you own the hottest clubs in L.A. and have starlets on your arm is only going to make some kids want to emulate you even more. You're perfect," she added, with a quick kiss to his cheek. "And I mean that in so very many ways."

He pulled her close, just wanting to feel her next to him.

"How about you?" she asked, snuggling closer. "Anything fabulous and new on the PR front?"

"Actually it sounds good," he said. "Joe's got some excellent ideas. More innovative than the group I've been using. Honestly, I was impressed. I'm going to meet with him and his team, but unless I've missed something big, I think I'm going to go with him. I need Heaven to launch with a huge splash, so I need the best on the job."

"Great." She wanted to be thrilled he had a plan in place, and for Ty, she was. But…

Without thinking about it, she sat up, frustrated and a little disturbed.

His fingers stroked her back, the simple touch calming. "Claire? What is it?"

"Nothing. I'm— Nothing."

"Doesn't look like nothing from where I'm sitting."

"Seriously. It's just something that's bugging me." Ty had already told her not to tell Bonita about Joe's pass at Claire, and since Joe's storeroom tryst had nothing to do with his PR skills, she imagined that Ty would simply think she was making a mountain out of molehill.

"Claire."

"Fine. Bonita caught him in a closet. With another woman."

His face registered shock. "She's sure? No misunderstanding?"

"No," Claire said, thinking about the image she'd seen on Bonita's phone. "I'd say she got it right."

"Well, forget it then. I'll keep working with the folks I already have on board."

"Really?" The announcement surprised her, especially the force with which it was rendered. "I thought you were all about freedom until she had a ring on her finger."

"As a general rule, sure. A guy shouldn't have to call a woman he's not committed to and tell her he's going out on a date with another girl. But come on. Once you claim someone as your girlfriend— even without a ring—screwing another girl in a closet at a party you're both at takes a particular brand of asshole."

He leaned over, reaching for his phone, even as Claire soaked in the statement, wondering where exactly she stood. Girlfriend material? Or on the Do Not Need To Call List.

"Hey, Lucy. I've got a guy named Joe set to call you for an appointment. Don't give him one. Tell him I'm sticking with the plan we've got in place. Thanks."

He clicked off and turned back to her. "Done," he said, that simple word making her think that she could fall in love with this guy.

"But you liked his ideas."

"I did. But I'm particular about the people I work with."

*Yeah. Definitely a danger-to-the-heart scenario happening here.*

She shifted, uneasy. Fearing she was falling too fast and didn't have anything to hold on to. "Are you hungry?" She slid toward the edge of the bed, only to be stopped by his arm on her hand.

"Claire?"

"I'm good," she said. "I'm great. I just never expected— I mean I know you didn't do it for me, but…I don't know. You just make my head spin."

"I know what you mean," he said, leaning in close for a kiss. "You make me spin, too."

She ran her fingers through her hair and finished sliding off the bed. She wanted it, this closeness, but Ty was a short-timer, and she needed to protect her heart. "You hungry?"

"Starved," he said.

"Then we really should have gotten take-out. I'll go check and see if the food fairies filled up the fridge while we were gone."

She padded toward the kitchen in bare feet, Hermione curling around her ankles as she walked, doing her feline best to trip Claire up. In truth, she was grateful for the cat, because concentrating on where she was walking meant she could ignore the noise in her head. A noise that said this could be the guy. That if they could get their lives to gel right, then this really could be the guy for her.

Just the thought scared her to death, because she'd never felt her heart move so fast before. And the truth was she barely knew Ty. And yet in some ways she already felt as if she knew him better than she knew any of her friends, including Joe, who'd been her only serious long-term relationship. Certainly she clicked with Ty better. They simply *fit.* Two peas in a pod, two pieces of a puzzle. Ham and cheese, biscuits and gravy.

And now, she thought, she really was getting hungry. "So, I'm looking in my fridge," she called, "and I have nothing and nothing."

He came into the kitchen and picked up the cat. "I'm in the mood for nothing," he said. "Maybe with a nice pesto sauce?"

"Wouldn't that be nice?" She closed the fridge and moved to the pantry. "Seriously, the cupboard is bare, and I need real food this time. Not that the strawberries and chocolate weren't exceptional."

As she watched, he gently untangled himself from the cat, then came into the kitchen and stood beside her as she peered helplessly into the void that was her pantry. "You've got a can of tomato-basil sauce," he said. "Any chicken?"

She made a noncommittal noise and opened the freezer. She started poking around, but he found the bag of frozen chicken breasts before she did. "Yes," she said, as he pulled the bag out. "I have chicken."

He grinned. "Go. Sit. Brush Hermione. But leave dinner to me."

"Seriously?" He'd managed to microwave chocolate, so she knew he had some culinary skill, but still...

"Two of my clubs have full restaurants," he said. "I'm not a chef, but I'm not clueless in the kitchen."

"You don't want any help?" Guilt at having her guest cook for her was warring with a little voice yelling *score!* simply from the reality that there was a man in her kitchen who knew how to cook.

"You can if you want. Or I can wait on you hand and foot."

"Put it that way," Claire said, then eased back toward the table. "I'll just watch."

"If you're going to play voyeur, you at least have to open another bottle of wine."

"*That* I can do," she said, and as he began rummaging in her kitchen, pulling out a box of spiral pasta, a can of salmon and some too-squishy tomatoes, Claire poked around in her wine rack until she found a nice bottle of pinot noir she'd been saving for a special occasion. She opened the wine and poured them both a glass, then sat back to watch the show as he moved around in her kitchen with practiced efficiency.

"Where'd you learn to cook?"

"My mom," he said. "It was part of her plan to make sure I could at least earn an income even if I'd never make it as a doctor or a lawyer." He shot her a grin that made her stomach do flip-flops. "I only enjoyed it because I got to play with knives."

"She took the time to teach you to cook, but

didn't sit down and try to figure out why you couldn't read better?"

"That's my mom for you. Both my parents. Very involved in their own lives. Rather tunnel-visioned about everything else."

"What do they do?"

"My mom works in a bank, my dad owns a car dealership, and their hobby is sniping at each other."

"So how come you opened a club first and not a restaurant?"

He shrugged, looking completely comfortable in her kitchen as he found her barely used food processor and plugged it in, then tossed in the tomatoes, some basil, and a handful of nuts he'd found.

She lifted a brow.

"Trust me," he said. "And I did it because a club is easier. I started with no food, just drinks. All I needed was solid music, decent alcohol and a fabulous dance floor."

"And now?"

"Now, each new club has a kitchen with signature appetizers. It's taken a while, but I've come a long way." He pressed the button to chop the food, and she watched him, not willing to talk over the noise. When he released the button, he smiled at her.

"Now I'm doing exactly what I want to do. In my business life, everything is perfect."

"And in your personal life?" she asked, then immediately wanted to kick herself.

He paused his preparations, then shifted his body so he was looking at her straight-on. "Right now," he said, in a voice that made her want to melt, "my personal life is pretty near perfect, too."

Since she wasn't sure how to respond, Claire only smiled, then took a sip of her wine. At the moment, she thought, her personal life was pretty near perfect, too.

Less than an hour later, her near-perfect personal life was supplemented by a near-perfect meal. She wasn't at all sure how he'd managed it, but somehow he'd taken the various dregs from her kitchen and turned them into the most amazing pasta dish. "You're either really good or I was really hungry."

"I'm really good," he said, and from the way he was looking at her, Claire wasn't at all sure that he was talking about the food.

"Yeah," she said, lacing heat into her voice, as well. "I've noticed."

"Claire," he said, and that was all it took. Her name on his lips. The desire in his eyes. She couldn't get enough of him. She was like an addict, and right then she was so very desperate for another hit of him.

He took her hand and pulled her to her feet, then led her to the couch. "Dear God, you're beautiful."

She felt her cheeks warm from the compliment, even though right then she wasn't about praise. She wanted to feel him beneath her, this man who'd gotten into her head, into her life.

He drew her into a kiss filled with so much promise that she thought she would drown in it. And it wasn't just a kiss, but a full-body sensual assault, with his tongue teasing her ear, her neck. His hands caressing her breasts, sliding down over the yoga pants she'd tossed on. Everywhere making her tingle and itch with need until she couldn't take the sweet torment any longer. "Touch me," she begged. "Touch me now."

He didn't disappoint. His hand slipped between them, his finger finding her clit then stroking back to slide inside of her, so deep she gasped and arched back.

"That's it," he murmured. "Let go. I want to feel you come for me."

"Please." It was the only word she could manage, the only word that seemed to fit, and as she arched back—his hand still taking desperate control of her sex, stroking and teasing—his mouth bent forward, suckling her first through the material of the tank top, then using his teeth to push the scoop neck lower and close his mouth over her nipples. She gasped as a hot cord of pleasure seemed to shoot from her nipple all the way down to her clit, sending tiny shockwaves through her, like little previews of the pleasures to come.

"Come on, Claire," he whispered. "Now."

But she didn't want now. She didn't want to come again, even despite the way the feeling was building and building inside her, an explosion that was teetering on a precipice, ready to burst over the cliff like fireworks falling down, down, down into the Grand Canyon.

"Not yet," she whispered. "Inside me. Please, Ty, please, I need you inside me."

He didn't need further encouragement, thank God, and as she raised herself up on her knees, he slid his pants and briefs off.

"Condom," he said.

"Oh, crap." Because she didn't have one and she didn't want to wait and—

"Wallet." She realized he'd reached for his fallen pants and dug a condom out of the wallet and, really, that was worthy of a kiss. So she did, and while he sheathed himself, she ravaged his mouth, her tongue sliding deep, deep inside, in the hopes of giving him some really specific ideas as to what she was looking forward to. What she wanted right then.

"Bedroom?" he whispered.

But she didn't want to wait. He was right there, and she shifted, the tip of him teasing her sex, and she was so wet and she really, really couldn't wait.

"Carry me," she said, easing herself down and sheathing him, then gasping as he drew her in closer, his arms tight around her, and him tight inside her.

She sighed with pleasure, her own enjoyment heightened by the desperate surprise she heard from his lips. "Claire," he whispered when words came back to him. "Oh, God, Claire."

He thrust upward, and she met him, their bodies colliding together with the kind of force that could move mountains and was sure as hell moving Claire. "Harder," she demanded, the word a moan, a plea, and he cupped her rear and thrust up as she tossed her head back, overwhelmed by the pleasure of it all.

"Put your legs around me," he demanded, and she did, and then he was lifting her up, their bodies still joined, and she squirmed against him, overwhelmed by the intense eroticism of being moved so intimately. "Hang on," he said, then backed her against a wall. She gasped as he thrust again, and this time, she wasn't able to bend back to lessen the blow, and she absorbed all of it, all of him, and damned if she wasn't going to explode from the pleasure of it all.

"More," she demanded, her hands on his shoulders, her focus on the feel of him. His cock inside her, his hands firm around her waist. The soft skin of his shoulders, firm beneath her hands as his body stiffened and jolted, pistoning into her with bold determination as the pleasure between them built and built.

She wanted it. All of it. And she wanted more, too.

"I'm close," he whispered. "Claire. Sweet Claire, I'm close."

"Wait for me." She slipped her hand between their bodies, her fingertips grazing his penis as he thrust inside her, the pad of her middle finger stroking her clit. Her body tightened around him, the sensations too much to bear, and as he gasped and stiffened—as he lost himself utterly in an explosion of shockwaves—she was right there with him, her very soul shaking free and floating up, up above them, then looking down on the two interlocked bodies that seemed so damned perfect together.

"Holy wow," Ty said, his strong hands holding her back and pressing her tight against him. "Wow."

He gently laid her down, his own body on top of hers until he rolled gently over, letting his fingertips trace lightly over her belly.

"I'm thinking bed is highly over-rated," she said. "A couch is more than adequate."

"What else indeed?" he asked. "But I think I can make you see the value of a bed. If you'd let me try."

She swiveled her head to face him and saw the look of mischief on his face. "Again?"

"I just can't get enough of you."

"Funny. I feel the same way."

He climbed over her to stand up, then pulled her into a bridal-style carry. He took her into the bedroom and laid her down, and this time their lovemaking was slow and sweet, with Ty trailing soft kisses down her body until she couldn't stand it anymore. He straddled her and slid inside, then pumped with a slow, deep urgency, his eyes never leaving hers. Never closing, either, as if he didn't want to miss a moment of what she was feeling.

She exploded in his arms, and as the last shivers of the orgasm ripped through her, he held her tight, his lips brushing her hair, his words soft and gentle. And as she fell asleep, she not only felt protected, she felt loved.

It was a damn nice feeling, and it was one that

still lingered when soft movements beside her woke her up. She rolled over to find him sitting up, running his fingers through his hair as he sat there confronting the day.

She reached over and stroked her fingertips down his bare back. "Ty?"

He turned, then smiled at her. "Morning."

"You're already up?"

"Considering I'm my own boss and I have a naked woman beside me, I can't believe I'm saying this. But I have to go home, get changed and get to work."

She yawned and stretched, the fabulous languor she was feeling warring with disappointment that he had to go. "Not me. I'm simply a cog in someone else's wheel. I've got a social dinner with my boss tonight, and then I'm on vacation for another full week."

"Rub it in."

She flashed him an evil grin, then waggled her eyebrows just for good measure. "I did that last night."

"Yes, you did," he agreed, leaning in for a long, slow kiss. "Probably best not to remind me. I might never get out of here."

"Would that be so bad?"

"Actually, I could probably get used to it." Another quick kiss and he slid out of the bed, then tugged on his slacks. She watched, appreciating the way he looked both with and without clothes, then slipped a robe on and followed him out to his car.

"Do you want coffee? Something to eat on the road? I can scrounge up a crumb or two."

"I'm good," he said. "Stay much longer and I won't want to leave."

"At the risk of sounding girlie and needy, do we have any plans for—"

"Tomorrow?" he suggested, and she smiled.

"Exactly."

"The only plans I have are to see you," he said.

And that, she thought, was an absolutely perfect answer.

# 8

WHEN TY ARRIVED AT Matt's house, there were only two guys he didn't know lounging on the couch, and he vaguely wondered if perhaps there'd been a fire drill. He couldn't think of any other reason why the house would have transformed so dramatically, but he had to admit he liked it.

Yes, he was used to his privacy back home in California, but for the last six months, he'd been doing just fine living in Boys' Town.

Now, though…

Now he'd had a taste of not only Claire, but the way she lived. Relaxed and quiet in a house that actually felt like a home, despite the construction zones. He thought of his own house back in L.A., decorated by a woman he'd hired off the Internet with art that meant nothing to him and colors he hadn't picked out. He'd told Claire it wasn't a home, and he realized now just how much he'd meant what he said. He'd been in California for just shy of a decade and it still wasn't his place any more than Dallas was. Hell, any more than the North Pole was.

For that, he thought, he envied Claire. Not Dallas—not that—but that sense of belonging to both a town and to a house. He felt it when he was at her place. A connection. A grounding with the world. And although he was surprised to admit it even to himself, there was something compelling about the thought of having that kind of home base.

He wandered into the kitchen, certain that he'd find a beer in there, and he wasn't disappointed. He was pouring a Guinness when he heard the front door open.

"Yo!" Matt's voice echoed through the house. "Who's here?"

Ty stayed quiet, certain his friend would find him eventually. Sure enough, Matt's next stop was the kitchen. "Friends of yours?" he asked, hooking a thumb toward the living room.

"Figured they belonged to you."

They both peered out toward the two guys, now sprawled on the couch, watching football off the TiVo. "Look safe enough," Matt says. "Chances are someone knows them." He glanced at Ty's Guinness then reached into the fridge and got one for himself.

"So give it up, dude. You've got that look. Something's on your mind." He took a long sip. "Or maybe it's someone?"

"It is," Ty said, freely admitting what was undoubtedly obvious.

"And she's okay with all this?"

"All what? All me?"

"Your life, man. More pictures went up this morning."

*"Shit."* Frustration curled in his gut like a snake. "Dammit, why the hell can't they leave her alone?"

"The pics aren't bad. Just the two of you at the club. Then a few at the Starr Resort. But there's speculation that the role model for single dudes everywhere has finally settled down."

"After two dates?"

Matt shrugged. "Guess they're seeing the same thing in those pictures I saw when I looked at the two of you."

Ty couldn't deny it. "She's special. Dammit, I think she might be the one. She's sure as hell the only girl who's ever had me thinking like this."

"Like how?"

"About her. About us. And constantly." Good God, it was as if she'd bitten him with a fast-acting relationship virus, and now his entire perspective was shifting.

Matt shook his head. "You know I love you, but you don't have it in you to settle down. You're not a commitment guy. Look at your business. Look at your life. Every time one of your clubs starts doing well, you start up another. You've got an empire going, dude. You conquer, you get bored and you move on."

Something dark and familiar curled in Ty's gut. Because Matt spoke the truth. That was one reason they were always such good friends. "You do the same with women," Matt said. "All the way back to fourth grade. Remember Dana Harper?"

"I didn't feel about Dana the way I feel about Claire," Ty admitted, and there was a freedom to saying it out loud. To making this thing that had been growing inside him real and tangible. "She's…" He trailed off, wishing he had the words to explain to Matt the way he felt around Claire. From the first moment he'd seen her, it had been as if she'd flicked a switch in him, and every moment with her had built from there. Already, he felt alone without her by his side, but at the same time, he felt centered, knowing that she was waiting for him. He didn't know how to say any of that to Matt, though, so he said simply, "I want to make it work with her."

"You've known her for three seconds, dude."

"Yeah, I know." And even though he knew that most people would think he was crazy for feeling so strongly about someone he'd met so recently, to Ty, the fast burn was actually comforting. He sat down on the two steps leading up to the living room. "Did I ever tell you how I came to buy Heaven?"

Matt leaned against the wall, arms crossed over his chest. "I don't think you have."

"I had the money I'd saved, and I knew I wanted to open a club—that was what I was working for, right? The question was when and where. And how I could get a place for the right price, especially in Los Angeles. I knew I wanted to own it, so I needed some place cheap enough that I could cover the down payment, but wouldn't have a horrible mortgage, because I knew it would be a while before I turned solid profit."

"Makes sense. So?"

"So I was having a hell of a time finding a place that fit the bill. I looked everywhere. My real estate agent probably wanted to strangle me, and I was just some dumb kid with cash back then, and I think he was getting pretty damn tired of me. Finally, we got to the real bottom of the barrel stuff, and he said he'd heard about a property that was going to be condemned. He thought that maybe since I was so picky, I'd want to buy it for the land and then build to my own specs."

"And it turned out to be Heaven?"

"Yup. Turns out it really wasn't that bad off. We got the court to extend the time before condemnation, stepped in and fixed it up, and then got it re-inspected. It passed, and then I kept on fixing it up until I got the place the way I wanted it."

"Great story if we were watching a real-estate reality show, bro, but I'm not seeing the connection to this girl."

"I knew the second he pulled up in front of that building that it was the location I'd been searching for. It was like a kick to the gut, you know. And when we went inside, I got more and more sure. I've always thought it was a little like falling in love." He thought of Claire, about the way he felt around her. "And I still think I'm right about that."

"Fair enough," Matt said. "But let me now step in as the voice of reason. When you bought Heaven, you hadn't already bought and tossed fifteen clubs before. Also, your Claire is a woman, not a building, and you can't remodel her anyway you want. And you can't keep her just because you want her."

"What are you saying?"

"I'm saying that you have to face the fact that even if she's the perfect woman for you, you may not be the guy for her."

Matt's words chilled him, despite the fact that he knew his friend was right.

"All I'm saying is that if you really want this to work, you're going to have to stick with it through the rough patches. Like this deal with Murtaugh? You're all set to go to Paris in, what? Less than two months, right? You think she's going to go with you? From what I know of Claire Daniels, she's staying right here."

"I know," Ty admitted on a sigh. "Believe me, I've thought about it."

"So what are you going to do?"

"I don't know," Ty said, wishing there was an easy answer. "I really don't know."

"THIS HAS BEEN A REALLY nice dinner. Thanks so much for inviting me."

Judge Monroe waved Claire's words away. "Nonsense. I think we've moved beyond such silly social niceties, don't you?"

"Absolutely," Claire said, trying hard not to grin. She adored and admired Judge Monroe, and the idea that the brilliant woman considered her a peer was the biggest career compliment Claire could think of.

"And you've enjoyed your vacation?" The judge's brows rose. "Because I expect you back at full capacity next week. The pile of screeners on your desk is insane, and we may be getting the Boreman death-penalty appeal." Screeners were cases that were decided without oral argument, and part of Claire's job was to write the original opinion for the judge to review. Death-penalty appeals were a bigger deal. The entire office shut down except for work on the case. The cases happened fast and the staff worked hard, often through the night.

"I'm ready. And if anything happens early on Boreman, you know you can call me in."

"I know," the judge said. "Not to change the subject, but I spoke with a friend over at the ABA. He thinks you should chair one of the committees next year."

"Really?" Being a committee chair for the American Bar Association was a big deal. "What do you think? I don't want to spread myself thin my first year in private practice."

The judge patted her hand. "Exactly what I was thinking. Give him a call. Tell him you're honored, but that you want to focus on the job and the commitments you already have in place—you'll keep up the charity work, of course?"

"Absolutely."

The judge nodded. "Good. I'd shoot for the ABA in two to three years. And, frankly, you may want to focus more on state-based opportunities. If you're looking for a judgeship, the most logical step is an appointment by the governor, then run for re-election after your term is up. But you won't get appointed if he doesn't notice you."

"Good plan," Claire said, though her head was spinning. She *did* want a judgeship. But that was in the far future. And while she intellectually understood that everything she did now would impact that future goal, it was still hard to emotionally wrap her head around the fact that the literacy auction she was preparing actually impacted her chance down the road to reach that ultimate goal.

The waiter appeared with their desserts and coffee, and after the judge took a sip of her coffee, she peered at Claire over the rim of the cup. "Now, let's discuss the issue of you getting noticed."

Claire swallowed the bite of crème brûlée, then nodded. "Well, although I'm not doing it for that reason, it occurred to me that the literacy auction

I'm doing in a few weeks serves that purpose. The right kind of publicity. Community involvement. That whole thing."

"Absolutely. But that wasn't the kind of attention I was referring to."

Claire licked her lips, the serious gleam in the judge's eye reminding her a little too much of her own mother's power stare. "That picture," she said. "From New Year's Eve."

"And the ones that followed," the judge said with a small nod.

"Right." She'd seen a few others that morning, but they had all been tame compared to that kiss. "Obviously I would have rather not had my picture spread all over the Internet, but there's not much I can do about it. And," she added with a lift of her chin, "I don't regret the actual kiss. Just the hoopla that followed."

The judge nodded. "I made a few inquiries about your Mr. Coleman," she said. "Quite the self-made man. He's also rather notorious. Particularly for the constant stream of women on his arm."

"I know."

"I'll be frank, Claire. It doesn't look good."

Her stomach clenched, and she focused on her dessert. "I realize that. Presumably that's why

Mr. Thatcher wants me to come in this week. A chat, he said."

"I'd say that's a safe bet." The judge reached across the table to squeeze her hand. "So that's my comment as your mentor. As your friend, though, I want to know how you feel."

"I like him," she said. "Actually, I more than like him. And the truth is, despite his reputation, I think he likes me, too."

The judge nodded sagely. "Please don't think I'm a prude. Personally, I'm glad you've found someone to go out with. To have fun with. But most people don't have their dating relationships splashed all over the Internet."

"I know." She drew in a breath. "But despite this little scandal, he's a good man. And I like him. I more than like him." She thought about Ty's reputation for being a party machine, but she'd never once got the impression he cheated. Certainly his reaction to Joe's tryst in the closet was proof of that. Everyone thought Joe was such a catch, and if she'd been locked in a clench with him, no one would have blinked. But the fact of the matter was that Ty was the better man. And yet he was the one who could damage her shiny reputation. It really wasn't fair.

"Will it lead anywhere?"

Claire licked her lips. "What do you mean?" she asked, though she feared she already knew the answer.

"If a relationship with a man like Ty will lead somewhere—a house, children, a family—then ultimately there's no harm to you. You're the woman he fell for, and by default you must be spectacular." The judge's eyes flashed with mirth. "Not fair, perhaps, but that's perception.

"But if it simply ends—if this is a tabloid romance between the two of you..." She trailed off and sipped her coffee. "Well, those types of stories can follow a politician around for years. So my question is, will this thing you have going with Mr. Coleman lead somewhere?"

Claire drew in a breath. "I don't think so," she whispered. "I'm really afraid that it can't. Not in the end. Not with what he wants to do. What he wants to be." She might desperately want to go down the path with him, but she was a smart woman, and she could see the end of the road from here. They'd have fun together for the next couple of months. Mind-blowing, fabulous, amazing fun. But then it was all going to fizzle out. He'd be in Paris or Hong Kong or who-knows-where, and she'd be here. And ten years from now when she was in front of the

Senate for an appointment to a Federal District Judgeship, someone would mention the fling and shoot her chances all to hell.

Just the thought depressed her.

"Claire…" The judge's voice was gentle, and not for the first time Claire said a silent thank you to the universe for giving her this woman, who had managed to become a friend, a surrogate mother, a role model and a boss all rolled into one.

"It's just…" She sighed, frustrated. "It's just that I don't want to give him up, you know?"

The judge's smile was wistful. "I know."

"How can I do it?" she asked, more to herself than to the judge. "How can I break away from something I want? From some*one* I want?"

"You think about what else you want," Judge Monroe said. "And then you decide if they mesh."

"And if they don't?"

"Then, Claire, you have to decide what you want more."

TY STIFLED A YAWN as he walked the perimeter of Heaven with Xavier, his landscape artist. The sun was barely peeking over the horizon, and he considered himself lucky that he'd found a guy willing to work the kind of hours Ty needed to put in to get the club off the ground in time. He'd spent most of the night at Decadent, then come over here about three to go over the checklist for the interior of the club until his dawn meeting with Xavier. After the landscaper left, he'd swing by his office for a few hours, check in with Lucy, then meet with the project's publicist to discuss the current campaign. He didn't intend to steal any of Joe's ideas, but the other man had definitely got Ty thinking, and he wanted to tweak the program a bit.

"We can do annuals along the walkway," Xavier was saying, "but I think you'll be happier with perennials. I brought some photos of a few other places I've done. Thought we could go over that and see if we're on the same page. Other than that, we've got the gravel and flagstone being delivered tomorrow, along with several yards of topsoil. Except for figuring out the border, we're all set."

"Then let's see what you've got," Ty said, following the man to his truck.

After pouring over dozens of photos of flowers, they finally decided to go exclusively with native plants, which Xavier assured him were not only beautiful but durable and low maintenance. "Tomorrow then," Ty said, as the landscaper drove away.

He locked up, running mentally through his

checklist, then got into the Ferrari and headed toward the office. He'd gone only three blocks when he realized he'd pushed the speaker on his phone and was dialing Claire. He hadn't even realized what he was doing—hadn't even realized she'd been at the forefront of his thoughts. But she had been. Hell, how could she not?

He shook his head, half exasperated, half amused and more than a little in love.

*Yeah,* he thought. *In love.*

And honestly, it felt pretty damn nice.

After a few rings, her voice mail picked up. He listened, soaking up the sound of her voice, until the beep. "Hey, it's me. Sorry. I wasn't thinking about the time. Hope I didn't wake you." He clicked off, smiling, and counting down the hours when he could see her again.

Unfortunately, the smile disappeared when he reached his office. "Your mom called," Lucy said. "And that guy you said was going to call about the thirty-minute appointment? He's really not happy that he's not getting his time."

"He'll have to learn to live with disappointment," Ty said, thinking of his mom. He'd have to call her back. As unpleasant as that reality was, he couldn't see another way around it.

Damn.

"He's in your office," Lucy said, the words sending a cold flash of anger down his spine.

He closed his eyes and counted to ten. "Dammit, Lucy, what the hell were you thinking?"

"I'm sorry," she said, sounding genuinely contrite. "He blew past me. I swear. The only way to keep him out was to call the cops, and I didn't think you'd want that…"

"No," he said. "You're right. I'm not mad at you. But I am a little bit miffed at my current guest."

"I really am sorry, sir."

"It's okay, Lucy." It wasn't, of course, but that wasn't her fault. He could see well enough what had happened—Joe had barreled in and completely terrified the poor thing. "Buzz me in five minutes. Use the intercom. Tell me security's on its way up."

"You want me to call security?"

"No. Just say they're coming."

She nodded, and he went in.

"Joe," he said. "This is a surprise."

"It wouldn't have been if you had taken the meeting like we discussed."

"Good point," Ty said, settling in behind his desk. "What can I do for you?"

"You can give me the thirty minutes you promised me. I'd like the chance to prove to you that Power Publicity can get you to the top."

"I think I can get there on my own with a team I choose based on my own requirements. But I appreciate your concern for the health of my company."

"Dammit," Joe said, the last hint of professionalism dropping. "What the hell happened? We talked, it was good and then suddenly you're kicking me to the curb without a hint of a goddamned explanation."

"Let's just say that I was less than impressed with the way you treated your girlfriend," he said. "Fooling around in the storage closet? Not the kind of behavior I want from the man who's watching my public profile."

Joe's jaw dropped. "You're not giving me a chance because of *that?* For goodness' sake! Bonita forgave me, but you won't?"

"I'm surprised to hear that she did, actually," Ty said cooly. "But I'm not Bonita, and no. I won't."

Joe nodded, a muscle in his cheek twitching, his dark features seeming ominous despite the shafts of sunlight streaming in through the window. "Fine. Fair enough. Whatever." He stood. "But this isn't over, Coleman. Mark my words. This isn't over."

He left, slamming the door, and as Ty released a

frustrated breath, Lucy buzzed in. "It hasn't been two minutes. Do I still need to announce security?"

He chuckled. "No, Lucy. I think it's fine now."

"Oh. Good. Your mother's on the line."

"Thanks." *And the day was going from bad to worse....*

"As if that's the way I want to see my son," she said the moment he said hello. "Splashing that nice girl all over the Internet. Honestly, Ty. Sometimes you just don't think."

He cringed, hating the way she could turn him into a little boy again. "Great to hear from you, too, Mom. It was so nice seeing you at Christmas."

She paused, stumbling over her words, because they hadn't seen each other at Christmas. The topic hadn't even come up. Now she sighed, low and long. "You need to settle, Ty. You need to stop playing and settle down."

"What part of my career do you think is a game, Mom? The part that pays my bills? The part that lets me endow scholarships? The part that lets me travel? Or maybe it's the part that paid off your mortgage?" He'd thought that would help. Thought that maybe if he showed his parents that he was financially solvent—and responsible—that they'd stop looking at him as a cutup. But it hadn't happened. He didn't understand why his relationship with his parents was so completely screwed up, but he knew he hated it. More than that, as much as part of him wanted to simply run away from the relationship word all together, part of him craved a real one. A healthy one.

*Claire.*

He couldn't imagine her making him feel like an idiot or a failure or a man less than he was. And he sure as hell couldn't imagine her making their children feel that way.

Children? Where in the name of God did that come from? He forced the thought away, choosing instead to tune back into his mother's backpedaling, telling him that they appreciated the money, of course they did, they just wished that he'd earned it by a "less-sleazy means" than those "damned clubs. Honest labor, Ty. With your difficulties you should have gone into construction."

"Excuse me for living my life the way I want to."

"You want to be all over the papers? Want your girlfriend looking like a slut in front of the whole world? And a senator's daughter. Poor thing. She must be mortified."

Because that hit a little too close to home, Ty shifted. "Listen, Mom, it's been great talking to

you, as always, but I've got another call on the line."
He hung up, then sank down into his chair and
closed his eyes, hoping to hell that this would all
turn out all right. He never thought he'd say it, but
his mother was right—that bullshit with the blogs
couldn't be easy on Claire.

He'd dragged her into the muck. He only hoped
that she'd trust him to keep her from getting
sucked under.

# 9

"MR. THATCHER WILL see you now."

The receptionist's smile was both sweet and bland, which gave Claire no clue about what was going to happen in that office. Not that the receptionist would necessarily know her fate. It wasn't as if the firm would have circulated a "beware the slut" memo.

Then again, maybe they would, because she was certain that was the way that the firm now saw her, and all because of a few stupid pictures.

"Claire," Malcolm Thatcher greeted her at the door, his hand extended, as Errol Dain rose behind him. "Thanks so much for coming in today. We didn't mean to bother you during your vacation."

"I thought I should come in now instead of waiting until next week," she said. "I wanted to clear the air."

The two men exchanged glances. *Yep*, Claire thought. *I'm here about those pictures.*

"Have a seat, my dear. The truth is that we simply wanted to let you know that we're one hundred percent behind you."

"Definitely one hundred percent," Dain put in.

She nodded, but stayed silent, unable to allow the tiny bloom of hope to blossom.

"Mistakes can happen to anyone."

"Anyone."

"Certainly we in the law understand that."

"It's a question of *intent*," Dain said. "Certainly you didn't intend for those unfortunate photos to be made public."

"I didn't even intend for them to be taken," Claire said wryly.

"Exactly," Thatcher said, looking at Dain, who nodded as if Claire was a star pupil. "That's my point. Had you known, you wouldn't have gone there."

"So we'll simply chalk this up as a mistake in judgment."

The hope in Claire's stomach that had started to bloom curled up and turned brown. "Ty, you mean."

"I'm sure he's a nice man, but obviously you have a reputation to protect."

"As do you," she said, her voice flat.

"Of course."

"Right." She smiled, then stood up. "Well, I think

we're all clear here. I…well, I guess I'll see you both in July."

"Wonderful."

"We're looking forward to it."

"You're going to be a real asset to the firm, Claire. Someday, I expect you'll be an asset to the bench."

She drew in a breath, ambition swirling within her. "That's my plan, sir." And with the kind of experience she could get at a firm like Thatcher and Dain, she knew she'd be well on her way.

But as the men escorted her back to the elevator, she couldn't help but think about what she was giving up. *Ty.*

But there was no future in that man. And above all else, Claire was a woman who wanted a future.

As the elevator doors slipped shut, Claire closed her eyes on a sigh, then did the one thing she'd been holding back for the whole damn meeting: She cried.

SOMETIMES, CLAIRE THOUGHT, it sucked to be on vacation.

She stood in front of the microwave, Hermione in her arms, and waited for the popcorn to quit popping. If she were at the office, her mind would be fully occupied, with no room to think about Ty or her future or stupid Internet pictures.

Just Claire and the sweet bliss of being lost in the work without all the messy emotional stuff.

Not that she didn't have work she could do at home. With the literacy fund-raiser fast approaching, she had a pile of paperwork on her desk that needed to be updated, a to-do list a mile long, and a telephone waiting for her to burn up the lines seeking sponsorships and selling tables to corporate donors.

Lots of work.

Too bad she couldn't focus on it, what with the way her mind kept wandering to Ty.

Which probably meant it was a good thing she wasn't at work. She'd be fired in five minutes for a serious lack of concentration.

The microwave binged, sending the cat bolting out of her arms, and she jumped in surprise, then tensed when the phone rang. She'd ignored every one of Ty's calls yesterday, letting the machine pick them up. It was the wimpy way, she knew, and on the whole, Claire was not a wimpy girl. But right then, she'd had no choice. Her mind simply couldn't grasp the idea of picking up the phone and not inviting him over. She'd needed time to get her head wrapped around the concept that she had to nip this thing in the bud. As much as she loved being around him—as much as he made her feel alive—the simple fact was that he was ephemeral, and in less than two months he'd be little more than a memory. They both knew it, though they'd only ever talked around the reality.

Her career, however…

That wasn't ephemeral. It was rock solid. And it deserved—and required—her protection.

The machine picked up, and she heard her voice, then the beep, then, "Claire? Listen, it's Ty again. I don't want to harass you if you don't want to talk, but I'm starting to get worried here. Can you at least send me a text message and let me know you're okay? Then I'll only feel the pain of the stab in my heart because you're avoiding me, and not because you're passed out cold in a ditch somewhere."

She shook her head, amused, and decided at the last possible second to answer, almost missing him. "Ty?"

At first she heard nothing, then a sharp intake of air. "Claire. You're there. I've been worried."

"Yeah. About that. Look, I'm really sorry. I…I just…well, I just had some thinking to do."

"I'm hoping the fact that you're talking to me now means the thinking came out down on my side."

She closed her eyes and didn't say a word.

"Or maybe it didn't."

"Ty—"

"Don't say it. I don't want to hear it."

"It's just that you're going to leave." She hesitated, waiting for him to deny the inevitable, then closed her eyes when no response came. "You're going to leave," she repeated. "And I don't want to be a fling."

"I don't see you that way, Claire."

"Already I'm getting blowback. Those stupid pictures…"

"I'm truly sorry. But, Claire, we can work it out. I swear. You're not a fling to me."

"Are you going to stay in Dallas?"

"Lots of couples have long-distance relationships."

She hesitated, knowing this was it. This was that line in the sand everyone always talked about and she'd never yet toed up to it before. She had to now, though. If she didn't do it now, it would only get harder later.

"Some couples, sure," she said. "But not me. That's not for me, Ty."

"I see."

"I don't think you do," she said, frustration bubbling inside her. "You say you understand, but you don't. Not really. But there's no way we can have a real relationship, Ty, and I'm not interested in a fling—"

"I told you—"

"*No*. It's a fling by definition, don't you see?" Tears trickled down her cheeks, and she swiped them away, frustrated. "You leave, and I'm the one left holding the tattered shreds of my reputation."

"Claire…"

"I'm sorry, Ty," she said, her voice breaking. "I'm sorry. But I have to go now."

AND THEN SHE HUNG UP, and Ty was left staring at his phone, feeling like an idiot. He was still feeling that way fifteen minutes later when he wandered into the kitchen, ostensibly to get a beer, but really because he didn't know what else the hell to do with himself.

"You look lost," Matt said, looking up from the kitchen table where he was digging into a Big Mac and editing a brief.

"I feel it," he said, then gave his friend the rundown of his conversation with Claire.

"Shit," Matt said. "Sometimes I hate being right."

"I'm not particularly fond of it, either," Ty admitted.

"So what are you going to do now?"

Ty shook his head. Because what the hell could he do?

"You could stay. Buy a house. Hang here. Get on a plane when you need to and handle business elsewhere. Then come back home to the wife and kiddies and have Sunday-afternoon barbecues in my backyard."

"Since when do you have Sunday barbecues?"

"You manage to settle down, I'll manage to barbecue."

That at least earned a smile, and for that, Ty was grateful to his friend.

"So what are you going to do now?"

He took a long pull on the beer. "Not sure what I can do."

Matt put his pen down on the brief and looked up at Ty. "You? You're not sure? The guy who moved to Los Angeles with only the clothes on his back, and now has an empire that can buy my sorry ass a dozen times over. You don't know what to do next?"

"This isn't me playing hard ball to get a piece of real estate, Matt. This is a woman, and she's made up her mind."

"She's made up her mind she doesn't want a fling. Prove to her it doesn't have to be one. Hell, prove to her she can't live without you." Matt shrugged. "That's what I'd do, anyway. If there was a woman I cared enough about, I'd do that in a heartbeat."

"HOW ARE YOU DOING?" Alyssa asked, passing Claire a very full glass of wine, the label on which said THERAPY, and which Alyssa claimed she couldn't resist when she'd seen it at the grocery store.

"I've been better," Claire admitted. It had been three days, and she'd been unable to keep Ty out of her mind. Part of that was his fault. He had, so far, sent her something every hour, on the hour, from 10:00 am to 5:00 pm. Her living room was overflowing with flowers and candy, and he'd moved on now to season's passes to touring Broadway productions, sporting events and even gift cards for area boutiques and restaurants.

"I knew I should have fallen for a man with a bigger bank account," Alyssa quipped, after Claire outlined the extent of gift inundation.

"I can't decide if I should be annoyed or amused."

"Amused," Alyssa said, picking up a giant chocolate pig. "Definitely amused."

"It's pointless, anyway," Claire said, then took a long sip of wine.

"What do you mean?"

"He's doing this so that he's constantly on my mind." She shrugged. "Really not necessary. I can't think of anything else, dammit." She tilted her head back and sighed. "I can't believe I go back to work on Monday. I'm going to be completely useless." Thank goodness the Supreme Court had stepped in on the death-penalty case. At least she didn't have to try and wrangle articulate legal theory out of her lovesick head right away.

"Maybe you should see him? Try to work things out. Chris and I managed."

"We can't be what the other needs. He hates Dallas, and I don't want to live out of a suitcase. I can't. I have a career that I love that's barely even off the ground. I'm not going to toss it to be the girl who follows Ty around the world. Dammit! I almost wish we hadn't met. It's like…I don't know, if I did say that I'd go with him, it might be fun for a while, but then I'd start to resent it, you know? Ten years from now, when I have friends who are getting appointed to the bench or running their own firms or…"

"I know."

"Damn." She swiped at her eyes, hating that she was crying. Hating that her insides were a mess. "So, a movie. I just want mindless entertainment."

"I'm thinking not a romance."

"A movie where they blow shit up," Claire said. "Lots and lots of nonromantic destruction. That's what I want."

"We can do that," Alyssa said, then started thumbing through the on-demand channels. In no time at all, they were engrossed in the action, and all too soon, Alyssa was slipping her purse back over her shoulder, hugging Claire, and telling her it would all work out.

"Glad you're optimistic."

"We made a pact. It worked out for me, it has to work out for you. We have Karma."

"So far, I think Karma has been punking me."

"Faith," Alyssa said, then gave her a hug. "And think about what I said. Try to find some middle ground with the guy. You miss him, Claire. It covers you like a sheen."

"What does?"

"Melancholy."

Claire rolled her eyes, then held open the door. "And on that happy note."

She watched as Alyssa got in her car and drove away, then stood there, wondering what she was going to do now to avoid thinking about Ty. Unfortunately, nothing came to mind, and she ended up baking chocolate-chip cookies, which was reasonably diverting since she was a lousy cook and had to focus on the ingredients so as to not end up with a big pile of mush. She'd gone to the grocery store finally (the trip had reminded her of Ty) and she'd loaded her kitchen up with way more food than she needed simply because she'd used the trip—and her self-imposed cooking lessons—as a distraction.

She'd plowed through all of the pending work she had for the committee, with the exception of calling Ty to confirm the bachelor auction and ask about the celebrity involvement. At this point, she really didn't think she should ask.

She watched *The Maltese Falcon* while the cookies baked, but Bogie only made her sad. Then she gorged herself on five of the dastardly things, then took a book and crawled into bed. Honestly, brain mush or not, she'd be glad to get back to work. As it was, she was utterly useless.

The words were swimming on the page when the sharp tones of her phone on the side table jerked her awake. She snatched it up automatically, pressing the talk button without looking at the display.

"Claire."

His voice, so soft, so liquid, ran over her like warm water, and she could feel herself melting as if she were made of nothing more than spun sugar.

"Ty." She swallowed, trying to find her voice. "I should go. I was just about to fall asleep. I didn't mean to answer the phone."

"You're in bed?"

"Yes, I—"

"What are you wearing?"

"Ty, please don't." She needed to hang up. To end this. But somehow, she couldn't quite manage.

"Don't what? Don't imagine you there, snug beneath the sheets in an old t-shirt and a pair of pink panties?"

"Please…"

"Because I can. I can picture everything about you, Claire. Everything from the tiny flecks of gold in your chocolate eyes to the way that one lock of hair curls backward at your crown. I've memorized the freckles on your stomach, Claire," he continued, his words like a lullaby. "You have four that peek out just barely under the lace of your bra. And one that dances on the edge of your navel."

She tried to make a word, but couldn't quite manage it.

"Will you touch it, Claire? That sweet place were the freckle hides on your navel? Will you stroke it for me, just with the tip of your finger?"

"Yes," she said, even before she realized that her hand had already moved to comply.

"There's a birthmark on your inner thigh, too. Can you press a kiss to your fingertips? The other hand, and then slide your hand down, and give the mark a kiss?"

"I—"

"Please, Claire, I want to know my mouth is on you."

*Oh, Lord.* Her head was swimming, her body tingly, as she pressed a kiss to her fingertips, then found the tiny birthmark on her inner thigh.

"Did you do it?"

"Yes."

"Now slide your hand up until you just brush your clit. Are you wet?"

"Yes."

"What are you doing with your other hand? Is it still on your belly button?"

She shook her head, realizing she'd moved her hand up, and now it was kneading her breast, her fingers pulling and tugging on her nipple. And her hips were moving, too, as if by finding a rhythm she could urge her hand to climb higher.

"How do you do this to me?" she asked. "You just talk, and I turn to goo."

"Your hand, Claire. Where's your hand."

"On my breast."

"Is your nipple hard?"

"Oh, yes." Hard and desperate and longing for attention.

"I'm flicking my tongue over it. Can you feel that?"

She whimpered, and as that was all she could manage at the moment, he was just going to have to deal.

"Good girl. Now slip your hand between your legs." She did, the sensation almost more than she could bear. She was close, so close....

"That's me touching you. I can feel your clit, Claire. It's swollen under my tongue."

She could feel it. So help her, she could feel the pressure of his tongue. Feel the way it tied her up in knots.

"I'm licking. Sucking, and, baby, you taste so good."

"Don't stop," she begged, moving her own hand faster and faster.

"Never," he said as the sensations crescendoed within her. "Will you come for me, Claire? Will you com—"

*"Yes—"*

And as his words flowed over her, Claire arched up and cried out Ty's name, certain that she really could, in fact, feel his hands upon her.

# *10*

TY'S FINGERS ACHED with the need to touch her. To stroke her. To feel her tremble beneath him as she came.

But she was all the way across town, her naked body at the other end of a phone line, and him in his car in the parking lot behind Decadent, trying and failing to keep his mind on work and off the woman whose mere existence made him want to do nothing more than hold her and lose himself inside of her.

He'd seen the fall coming, but he could never have imagined the intensity with which he would descend, crashing down into the realm of mortals. The realm of men who wanted a woman—one single woman—who completed him like no one else ever could.

And the hell of it was, he didn't know how to have her. Didn't know the magical phrase that would make her become his. He'd told Matt once that this wasn't a negotiation, but at the time, he hadn't realized just how true those words were. And now all he could do was try to keep himself front and center in her thoughts, her heart, her mind.

*Sex.* And yet he wanted so much more than sex.

But every night for the past three nights he'd called her at bedtime. They'd fallen into a sensual rhythm, with his words an aphrodisiac between them. He'd caressed her with his voice, and imagined her arching up to meet his touch, her lips ripe, her body ready for him.

*Damn,* the mere thought made him hard, and he closed his eyes and drew in a breath as he whispered good-night to her, her soft moans and labored breathing making him desperate with need, and not even for sex. But for that connection.

"Claire," he whispered, because he had to tell her. Had to break his own self-imposed rule. "Claire, I miss you."

He waited, wanting to hear her response, but instead hearing only breathing.

And then—thank you, Lord, yes—a soft, whispered, "I miss you, too."

It did him in, and though she hung up the phone, avoiding any further chatter, he knew that he'd crossed a line. Made a dent. And, yeah, that gave him hope.

He fed off that hope for the rest of the day, then knew that he had to take it further. He had to see her. Had to convince her that they could be together, because it was hell for both of them being apart.

Somehow, someway, they could work this out. Except for his parents, he'd never once failed at something he'd set his mind to. And, to be honest, maybe he could even fix that parental rift if he really focused. But the point was he wanted her. She wanted him. And there had to be a way around, under or over this chasm that loomed between them.

He couldn't find it over the phone, though.

Time to move on to something else. Time, he thought, to bring out the big guns of romance.

SHE WAS LATE, and Ty was getting nervous. He'd spent the day dealing with Heaven's issues and consulting with Fred and looking forward to seeing Claire that night. Hoping that she *would* see him. But if she didn't even come home, that possibility was shot all to hell.

And if she didn't come home, then where the hell was she?

He forced himself not to consider the possibility that she was out on a date because, frankly, the idea was simply too, too depressing.

Instead, he waited. And waited. And waited some more.

When midnight turned to one in the morning, he began to think that maybe he'd have to give it up and go home. He was about to pack up the PDA he'd been reviewing documents on when he saw a pair of headlights turn onto the street. He held his breath, and then—yes!—a Volkswagen Beetle turned into the driveway and Claire slid out.

She didn't see him at first, too busy concentrating on getting her purse out of the car. She bent over, and he watched with appreciation the way her jeans curved against her body. He imagined her running her own hands over those curves, following his directions. And, yeah, he wanted to be the one doing the caressing now.

More than that, though, he simply wanted to hold her.

She hooked her purse over her arm, then took a step toward the door. One simple step before she halted, her expression wary. "Hello?"

He stood, at first unnerved, and then amused. Because she didn't see Ty Coleman. She saw a handyman in coveralls, a gimme cap and a paint-splattered toolbox. "Claire," he said. "It's me."

She paused, and the expression of pure delight

that he saw on her face rocketed through him. She could try to deny it with words, but he knew—he could *see*—that she wanted him there.

Her expression shifted, and she pursed her lips. "What are you doing here?"

"I was just getting ready to leave, actually. Then I saw you drive up."

She moved to the door and slid her key into the lock, glancing down as she did at the box filled with various supplies he'd picked up at Home Depot. "What on earth is all that?" She pushed open the door, then met his eyes. "How long have you been here?"

"Since eight," he said.

She blinked. Then she pressed her hand over her mouth. *"Eight?"*

He shrugged matter-of-factly. "I needed to see you, Claire."

Her expression softened. "Yeah. I know. Me, too." She closed her eyes and breathed in, and although his heart was leaping, he was certain the admission cost her. "Well, you better come on in. Chances are *The National Enquirer* is parked across the street, taking pictures."

He motioned to his workclothes. "Doubt they even know who I am. Just the local, very dedicated handyman here to look at your floors, ma'am."

"My floors?"

"I promised to teach you how to stain concrete."

He heard the soft intake of her breath, then his own name on a whisper. "That's…wow." Her voice broke, and she held the door open, ushering him in. "Just floors, though. I want us to be clear."

He stepped over the threshold. "What if I call you from the other room? Can we go beyond floors if we're both on speakerphone?"

"Ty…"

He pushed the door shut, leaving the box of tools and stains on the front porch. "I've missed you," he said, taking a step closer and praying she didn't back away.

"I've missed you, too," she said, holding her ground and answering his prayer. "But there are rules."

"I don't recall any contract. No fine print."

"When we…on the phone…we were setting up boundaries."

He reached out and stroked a single curl of her hair, letting the soft length of it caress his skin, the sensation so damned erotic he wasn't certain he could stay there with her. Not if she wanted him to behave himself. Because right then, behaving himself was the last thing on his mind.

"Ty? Are you listening?"

"I'm a rule-breaker, Claire. Always have been."
She licked her lips. "Well, I'm not."

"Maybe you should be." He stepped closer.
"Break a few rules with me, Claire. I promise, you
won't regret it."

Her eyes met his, and the sadness he saw there
just about did him in. "Can you promise me that?
Because already I have regrets. I don't want to,
dammit. I don't want to regret a minute with you,
but—*damn*." She turned away, moving into her still-
a-war-zone of a living room, while he stood, a bit
shell-shocked, not at all sure where to go from there.

All he knew was that he couldn't stand to see her
so miserable, and he went to her, putting his hands
on her shoulders, then pressing his lips to her ear. "I
would never do anything to hurt you. Or make you
regret. *Never.* So tell me, Claire. Do you want me to
go?" He didn't want to, but if that's what she needed,
then damn it all, he'd walk right out that door.

He felt the rise and fall of her shoulders as she
drew in air, then stiffened, apparently coming to a
decision. "No," she said, slowly twisting around to
face him. "I don't want you to go. I've missed you
so much, but we can't do this. How can we do this?"

"Easy," he said, leaning forward, her lips seeming
to beckon him on. "We do it like this." He brushed

his lips over hers, softly, giving her time to pull away, but desperately hoping she wouldn't. Some guardian angel somewhere was looking after him, because she didn't bolt. Just the opposite. She opened herself to him hungrily, her mouth claiming his, her arms going around him and pulling him in close.

"I MISSED YOU," she said. "So help me, Ty, I've really missed you."

"I don't know how I stood not being able to touch you," he said, and his words floated over her like warm honey. For so many nights now she'd been fantasizing his hands on her body, and now he was there, right there in her arms. And although she knew it was stupid and crazy and possibly a career killer, right then she didn't want him anywhere else. As much as it would kill her when he left—as much as any public hint of their relationship could rip her career to shreds—it didn't matter. All that mattered was *this* moment. *This* man.

She didn't know if that made her irresponsible or merely human. She didn't much care.

"Rules," she said, pushing gently away, almost done in by the longing she saw on his face, his eyes reflecting back what was in her heart. "This time, there really are rules, Ty."

"Anything. Right now, I'd pretty much agree to anything."

She laughed. "I'll keep that in mind for when I get you naked. Right now, I just want to lay down the ground rules."

His brows rose. "Shall I call a notary?"

She grimaced. "You're funny. Now knock it off so I can tell you."

He brushed a kiss over her nose. "Thank God you let me through your door," he said, and although she silently seconded the thought, all she said was, "I let you in because you had stuff for my cement. I expect new floors, you know. Otherwise we're talking a serious bait-and-switch."

"I'll keep that in mind. Although I should probably get brownie points for Tawny Martin," he said.

"Excuse me?" Tawny Martin had won an Emmy for her work the previous year on one of the season's most popular television shows. "Are you saying what I think—"

"She'd be happy to do the auction. Her son has a learning disability. It's a pet cause for her, and she has ties to Dallas. Her sister lives here."

"Ty! Thank you!" She pulled him into a big hug, then gave him a rock solid kiss. "MJ will be ecstatic."

"Just so long as you are," he said.

"Believe me. I am."

"So can we forget the rules?" he asked, hopefully.

She stared him down. "Rules," she said firmly. "No blogs or papers or Tweets or anything. No pictures. We show up in any sort of compromising position, and it's over. Some reporter starts shooting down my chimney, and it's over. I can't do that." She closed her eyes, thinking about the way it felt to have seen the picture of their kiss. The uncomfortable curl in her belly when everyone she'd ever met in her life sent her an e-mail. Even the one's with simply "you go, girl" messages had freaked her out. It wasn't that she couldn't handle the limelight, but if she was going to be photographed, it was going to be because she'd just been elected judge, or was debating her opponent or had just won a high-profile appeal.

Not because she stood on her tiptoes when she kissed.

"I think we can comply with your parameters," Ty said. "Should we buy disguises?"

"What?"

"You know. Wigs. Trench coats. Fake moustaches. So we can go out into the world incognito."

That time, she laughed even harder. "God, I have really missed you." She hooked her arms back around his neck, and pressed her body up closer. "I think we can skip the disguises. All we need to do is stay inside. Personally, I think the bedroom is the perfect place to hide to avoid the press."

"Sweetheart," he said, scooping her up into his arms. "I like the way you think." And with Hermione twining between his ankles in her own version of a welcome-back, Ty carried her to the bedroom, thankfully not tripping despite the eager feline.

"Sorry, cat," he said, toeing the door shut. "No one else allowed in here. How do we know there's not a camera on your little kitty collar."

"Bite your tongue," she said.

His grin was pure deviousness. "You bite it for me," he said. And, so help her, she did. Their kisses were wild. Their clothes removed with a fierce abandon, because, dammit, who cared about seams and stitches and cotton or silk when it had been days—*days*—since they'd seen each other. It was hedonistic, and wild and wonderful, and when he slammed inside of her, both of them so desperate their clothes still hung on arms and legs, she cried out with the force of the orgasm that crashed over her, so much more powerful now that it was the man himself touching her—filling her—and not just memory and desire and fantasy.

They collapsed together, sweaty and breathing hard, and grinned at each other. "We're good," Ty said. "We can make this work, Claire."

Damn, but she hoped that was true. "Rules," she said, again. "We follow the rules, we see what happens. I'm not jumping into the deep end, Ty. Not with my career. Not with my heart."

He took her hand, stroking the pad of his thumb over her skin. "We go however fast or slow you want. Whatever you want, Claire. You just have to say."

But that wasn't true, she knew, because what she wanted was for him to stay in Dallas. Right then, though, she was content with him staying through the night. For now, they could take it one day at a time. For now, they could hide in her house and pretend like real life and the press didn't exist.

It was a nice fantasy, and now that Ty was back in her arms, it was one she was happy to indulge. She didn't want to be the girl who had a fling, but she didn't want to be without him, either.

*Sometimes, you do have to step away from that line in the sand.*

"You're thinking," he said, stroking her cheek.

"Sorry. I promise I'll stop. Or try to, anyway."

"Maybe I can help," he said. He gently rolled her

over and straddled her, then traced his finger from her chin all the way down to her navel, and Claire had to admit that his plan was working. And when he dipped his mouth to follow the path of his finger, she couldn't even admit that. Because the thoughts in her brain were such utter mush that she couldn't even recall what they'd been talking about.

She wasn't even Claire anymore. She was just want and need and lust, and it was Ty who was giving that to her. Ty who was making her whole, filling her up.

It was Ty that she loved.

And right then—for that single moment—that would have to be enough.

IN THE END, it turned out that the guys Ty hired made the whole staining concrete process look one hell of a lot easier than it really was. About the only upside to the whole messy, multiple-day experience was the time spent in sweaty close quarters with Claire, and the fact that she now looked at him like a hero every time she stepped into her living room.

"It's so pretty I shouldn't put the furniture back," she said.

"No problem. I'll just give Goodwill a call. I'm sure they can haul all this stuff away."

"Soon they will," she said. "I furnished in early American thrift so I could buy real pieces once the walls and floor were done." She grinned up at him, her expression like Christmas. "Want to go to the furniture store?"

"You little vixen," he quipped, which had her rolling her eyes. "Yes," he said more seriously. "I'd love to."

In the end, they went together, him in a baseball cap, and her in big sunglasses and her hair in a pony-tail. It was ridiculous—if anyone was really paying attention they'd undoubtedly recognize them—but the charade made Claire feel better, just like the fact that she'd given him a clicker for her garage door, so that now he could park inside and walk in through the house, bypassing the front door all together.

"Have you talked to your parents?" she asked as they were getting close to the store.

He glanced her direction, surprised. But she'd turned and was looking out the side window, making her expression unreadable. "Some," he admitted. "My mom. She thinks I've ruined your life and that my job is unworthy. It wasn't a pleasant conversation."

"I'm sorry," she said. "I shouldn't have brought it up. It's just…" She trailed off. "Never mind."

"Wait," he pressed. "What?"

"It's just that if you're wanting to avoid Dallas because of them, I thought that perhaps there might be some way for you guys to mend fences."

"I don't think so," he said. "Sometimes, things are lost causes, no matter how much you don't want them to be."

Her lips pressed together in a tight line. "Like you staying."

Her words twisted through him, their sharp edges slicing and dicing him. "Claire—"

"No. It's okay. I understand. But it's a big town. You could be here years and not even know they're in the same city. You've already been here six months and haven't seen them, right?"

"It's not just them. I have things I want to accomplish. Things outside of the corners of this city."

"I take it commuting's not an option."

"I don't think there's a five-o'clock shuttle to Frankfurt," he said, then reached over and took her hand as he waited for the light to change so that he could turn into the furniture store parking lot.

"Never mind," she said. "I'm breaking my own rules, aren't I? Getting all serious and needy."

"I don't mind," he said softly. "I need you, too." And although they didn't solve anything, Ty thought the possibility of finding a middle ground was coming closer. It was almost as if he could reach out and touch it. It was there, he knew. It had to be. Because he wanted it so desperately, he couldn't even fathom the possibility that there was no way for them to make this work.

Although they may not have solved their relationship issues, Claire's furniture issue was wrapped up in record time, and by lunch the next day, she had a fully furnished living room and was dragging him off to small, funky shops to find local art and knickknacks to bring the room to life.

The days and nights were like a whirlwind, especially now that Claire was back at work during the day and he was working nights at Decadent and any time that he could squeeze in at Heaven. And although Claire's job was rather cush for an attorney, with a traditional nine-to-five schedule, she was also putting together the fund-raiser, and her evenings were often filled with a variety of phone calls regarding various auction items or catering emergencies.

On the whole, the scene at Claire's house was downright domestic, and Ty had to admit he liked it. More than that, he had to admit that for the first time in his life, he actually wasn't looking forward to leaving Dallas. It felt good going back there at the end of his workday. Welcoming. Not like his childhood home where he'd felt like he needed to sneak in and then go hide in his room until he could escape the next morning. No, Claire's house was a home, and he'd settled into its two thousand square feet one hell of a lot better than he'd ever settled into the six thousand square feet he had back in Los Angeles.

All about perspective, he thought. That, and the woman beside you.

He couldn't imagine a time when he'd ever be tired of her. So far, they'd run the gamut in conversation, covering everything from movies to television to the benefits of backyard box gardens to whether *Firefly* or *The X-Files* was more enduring. They laughed and joked and made love and Ty was certain that if someone pinched him, he would realize it was all a dream.

He really hoped no one would be cruel enough to pinch him.

"So I was counting my pennies," she said one night as they were lazing in bed. "And I don't think there's any way I'll be able to win your auction."

Said auction was the next day, and Ty would be lying if he didn't admit to being at least a little bit nervous. "I could lend you the money," he said.

"You most certainly could not! That's cheating."

"Is it? The money all ends up in the same place."

"Ty, you could outbid anyone who's likely to come to this thing. That's like rigging the thing. Not happening."

He lifted his hands in surrender. "Fine. No problem."

She shot him a sideways glance. "Just don't like whoever wins more than you like me."

He laughed and pulled her close. "No worries there. Do I at least get the honor of taking you to the ball, Cinderella?"

She pressed her lips together, and he held his breath, hoping she was ready to back away from her edict that they avoid public outings together as a way of preventing any more media snafus. This time, however, lady luck wasn't on his side.

"Us together at a charity function after all those photos?" She shook her head. "It looks too much like a date."

"It *can* be a date."

She shook her head. "Dammit, Ty, let's not do this. We both know dating isn't going to go anywhere for us. You're leaving, in case it had escaped your notice. And the whole world damn well knows it. And I'm not willing to be just one of your harem in the press. I'm just not. So don't even ask me to go there."

"Fine," he said, surrendering. "I'll just shoot you heated glances across the dance floor."

"Good," she said. "I'll be doing the same near the chocolate fountain." She leaned over and pressed a kiss to his cheek. "I'm sorry. I know it's a pain, but it's important to me."

"You could travel with me, Claire. Come to Europe. Spend time with me on the road."

"And practice law when?"

"The Internet's a wonderful thing."

She shook her head. "I require an office. Hell, I require a home base. Seriously, I don't work well when I travel. And more than that, my career is here. The reputation I need to build is here. No one in Italy gives a flip if I'm elected to a county judgeship." She cocked her head. "Why don't you stay here? Buy a house. Utilize that amazing invention called the Internet, and only rack up frequent flier points when you absolutely have to."

"Claire…"

"Hard isn't it? Having the voice of reason tossed back in your face?"

"Eventually," he said. "Eventually we're going to come together on this."

Her mouth curled into a smile, and she kissed

him. "I hope so. Because I'm beginning to wonder how the hell I ever lived without you."

"Believe me, sweetheart," he said, pulling her in close, "I know the feeling."

# *11*

TY MIGHT BE THE ONE being auctioned off, but Claire was a wreck. An absolute wreck, and she paced the back of the ballroom, trying to keep all of her nervous energy under control. So far, the fund-raiser had gone amazingly. The bids for lunch with Tawny Martin had topped the two thousand dollar mark, and all the other silent auction items had been snatched up at great prices. Claire had even already given her speech, so it wasn't as if she had that to be nervous about.

And now Ty was up there, talking so eloquently about the challenges he'd faced growing up, and she was so damn proud of him, and she was seriously—*seriously*—regretting not letting him fund her bid, because she was pretty certain she was going to have to jump whoever won the auction behind the building, just to keep the shameless hussy's mitts off her Ty.

He wrapped up, and MJ climbed onto the podium, and then before she could stop it, the bidding had begun.

From a charitable point of view, the event was a success, as the number kept growing and growing.

From the point of view of Claire's nerves, nothing had ever been more horrible.

As the bidding rose higher, his eyes searched the room, the steely purpose softening when his gaze landed on her. She felt that tug, a possessiveness. A claiming. And she couldn't help the wave of pure, green jealousy that flowed through her.

*Get a grip, Claire. You're not a couple. He's leaving. Sooner or later, he's going to be someone else's anyway.*

That was an empirical fact. And yet at the moment, all Claire wanted was to change it. To make it not so.

And when a date with Ty at that Friday's grand opening of his club, Heaven, was won by a lanky blonde in a skintight black dress, Claire was the only one in the room who didn't clap. Instead she stood there, her hands mere inches apart, and realized that she couldn't do this.

Not the auction—she could handle that.

But *this*. The parting from Ty. The not being a couple.

It wasn't enough to say location was the problem. At the end of the day, life was about life, and love, and all that gooey stuff. She needed Ty beside her to feel alive. And as for her career—well, she wasn't portable, but she could adjust.

She simply needed to figure out how.

TY HAD TO HEAD STRAIGHT to Decadent after the fund-raiser, so Claire didn't see him after the auction other than from across the room. She'd waved goodbye, and tried to convey with her eyes that she was going to figure something out, but she doubted he got the message. Significant looks might work in movies and books, but in life they were most often missed altogether.

Despite not seeing him, she was in a fabulous mood when she arrived at her office. She'd made a decision to figure out a way to work it out with Ty, and just knowing that she was aiming for that goal made her bounce and hum, and she entered the judge's chamber, whistling whatever tune had been playing on the radio in her car. She'd expected Myrna, the judge's secretary, to give her grief, but there was no one in the reception area. Frowning, she tapped on Judge Monroe's office door, then entered when she heard her mentor's crisp invitation.

Myrna was in there, and they both looked at her as she stepped inside, their expressions grave.

"What's going on?"

"Close the door, Myrna," the judge said.

"Judge Monroe…" Claire was starting to get nervous. In Judge Monroe's chamber, a closed door was never good.

"Have you checked your e-mails this morning? Any of the social sites you go to?"

She shook her head, dread building. "Why?"

"Come around here," the judge said, pointing to the screen and moving away from the desk as if to give Claire privacy. *Not* a good sign, and it only got worse when she was actually able to see what was on the screen: Her and Ty, in full porn-star mode, making love against the wall of the elevator in the Starr Resort parking lot.

She tried to speak and realized her hand was over her mouth. She forced it away. "How… Who… Oh my God, I'm so sorry."

The judge's brows lifted. "Sorry? Claire you haven't a thing to be sorry about except for poor judgment. Beds and bedrooms were invented to avoid that kind of thing."

"It's my fault," she whispered. "I didn't want to wait."

"Claire," the judge said sharply. "It is not your fault. The culprit is Joe Powell, at least if a young woman named Bonita knows what she's talking about."

Claire's head snapped up. "How do you know?"

"She called earlier. Myrna talked to her. Apparently she was hysterical. She said she'd broken up with him because of the way he fooled around and what he did to you. Naturally, Myrna asked what she meant by the last—"

"And that's how you learned about the picture."

"I'm afraid so."

Queasy, she glanced back at it, rage against Joe boiling inside her. She almost pulled her phone out. Almost called him. But she didn't. There were a lot of Joe's out there, and she couldn't call every one of them every time something horrible showed up on the Internet. Basically, she needed to learn to deal.

She drew in a breath. "Well, at least I don't have cellulite."

"What do you need?" the judge asked, and despite everything—despite the horror, and the humiliation and the complete mortification—all she wanted right then was Ty.

She hated that Joe had done such a horrible, cruel, embarrassing thing, but she did have to thank him for solidifying her feelings about Ty. Because right then, the stupid picture could go take a leap. All she cared about was the man.

"I see," the judge said, a grin pulling at her mouth. The woman always was too damn good at reading Claire's expressions. "You'll have to introduce me. I think this man may be even more remarkable in person than he is on paper."

"I will." She gnawed on her lower lip, then gestured toward the screen. "I—I feel like I let you down."

"I'm sorry you feel that way," the judge said. "Because you haven't. And the only way you could would be to hide under a rock and not confront it. To ignore it, and not learn from it."

Claire thought of Ty. Of getting to his side, fast and furious.

And she thought of one thing else she had to do before that.

"Don't worry," she said. "I've learned a lot. I promise."

HE COULDN'T GET a hold of her. Her voice mail was full, dammit.

Goddammed pornographic pictures and he couldn't get a hold of Claire and tell her—what? That he was sorry? For the act itself, he wasn't sorry at all. And Ty hadn't had a thing to do with getting that picture up on the Internet, so what the hell did he have to be sorry about?

Nothing.

But he hated that Claire had to see it. Had to feel it. Had to know that people all over Dallas were now looking at her differently.

They'd done nothing wrong, with the exception of not thinking about the damn security cameras in the elevators.

No, there was a real culprit this time, and as he once again looked at the phone note Lucy had handed him, he felt his entire body clench with rage, a rage he was currently burning by shooting down the Stemmons freeway at a speed that was not only illegal but was probably rather idiotic.

"Dammit." He slapped the steering wheel and slowed the car, not willing to drag some innocent bystander into his personal glimpse of hell.

Because that's what this was. If photos of a kiss had almost made Claire bolt, then *Penthouse* quality photos were probably going to make her crawl into a cave.

There wasn't a damn thing he could do to make it better, but he knew what the hell he could do to at least make himself feel better, and he whipped off the highway, following Lucy's explicit directions to a T.

Within ten minutes, he was in the elevator on the way up to the Power Publicity offices. Within fifteen, he was being shown to Joe's office.

And by the twenty minute mark, he'd punched the bastard hard in the nose. "Stay out of my life," he said. "Stay away from Claire. You pull another stunt like that, and I'll really make it hurt. Trust me when I say that I know enough of your clients that I can ensure a significant drop in your business."

And then he left, the staff standing as he did, and Joe left behind, holding a bleeding nose.

Might not be a perfect solution, but at least he felt better.

With Claire, though, he didn't think he could resolve his feelings quite so efficiently. With Claire, it was messy and hard, and he knew damn well she was going to try to lock him out. And that's why he was doing the one thing she wouldn't want him to do—he was heading straight toward her house to wait for her.

Fortunately, Malcolm Thatcher was in that day, because Claire wasn't certain her courage would last. But she had a piece to say, and she was saying it right now even if she had to speak into his security system and have the guards play it back for him.

"Claire," Malcolm said, meeting her in the reception room. "Is everything all right?"

"Have you seen today's entry on the blog circuit?" she asked, and could tell the answer simply by the way his face clouded. "Yes, well, that's why I'm here. Can we talk in your office?"

"Of course."

He led her back to the pristine corner office, and offered her a seat. She declined, preferring to speak standing up. The trouble was, she hadn't rehearsed what she wanted to say. She'd come straight over, her head filled with so many ideas of what to do, and now she had to sort through them all on the fly.

"Yes, well, here's the thing," she began. "A very smart woman once told me that I had to make a choice. I had to figure out what's important to me. And that's something I already know. Always have. It's appellate law. I've always loved it."

"Well, we're very gratified to hear that," Mr. Thatcher said. "But—"

She held up a finger. "No, hear me out. I love it. And I will practice it. I'd like to do that here, but if that's not possible, I can always find another firm. Let me be clear, too. This isn't a question of you asking me to leave because of that stupid photo from this morning. It's also a question of you asking me to leave because of *any* photos. I'll grant you the one in an elevator was a doozy, and I'm taking full responsibility, but a photograph of Ty and me kissing? And you get all bent out of shape because he's dated a lot? I'm sorry, but that has nothing to do with my skills as a lawyer. So unless you want to ask me to leave, please don't ask me to avoid the papers and the blogs. Because I can't. Not and still be around Ty. And I will be around him. Because even more than appellate law, he really is the one thing I want most in the world, and I'll not have my behavior monitored and judged by people who really have no business addressing the subject."

Malcolm nodded. "Very well. Then I wish you two all the best."

Claire held her breath, trying not to show her disappointment at what was so clearly a brush-off.

"Of course, I hope you feel comfortable enough with us to stay at the firm, and that you'll allow us to rescind what was undoubtedly an ill-planned request for you to stop dating Mr. Coleman."

She shook her head, as if that would make the pieces fall into the proper places. "Here? Wait. What? You're not rescinding my offer?"

"On the contrary. You've only firmed in my mind the skills that attracted us to you in the first place. Passion. Persuasion." He stood up and extended his hand. "Enjoy the rest of the term with the judge. This will blow over, Claire. These things tend to do that."

He was right, she thought. Scandal faded.

Love, though—it lasted forever. And so did a life. A relationship. Or, at least it did if you nurtured it right.

And that was something Claire intended to see to right then. Because she didn't want to wait even one more moment to begin sharing her life with Ty.

This time, though, she thought about what to say on the drive home. She'd call him up and invite him over, and as soon as he arrived she'd lay it all out for him. Because the truth was, she was willing to compromise. Willing to do almost anything, actually, if it meant that they could be together.

She only hoped he was, too. Because it was that 'almost' that was key. And unless they each gave a little, they'd never end up together. And the fact that such a horrible possibility was looming out there scared her to death.

She didn't see his car when she pulled up, but that wasn't unusual, since she'd given him access to the garage. And sure enough he was sitting at her kitchen table when she walked inside.

"Claire," he said, rushing to stand. "I'm so sorry. I—"

She hushed him with a finger to his lips. "I've been thinking, and have something to say. I can live with my picture in the paper and on blogs. Maybe not like today—I'd like the pictures to be more G-rated—but so long as it's clear who I am and where I stand in relation to you, then I'm okay. But it only works if we're together. Really together. I'm not interested in enduring that kind of humiliation for a fling."

"You know I want more," he said.

"So you say, but what I can't have is a relationship with a man who isn't there."

His brow creased. "I'm here, Claire."

"Not when you're in Dubai or Australia or Paris, you're not. And the thing is, I can't leave Dallas. I don't want to. It's home." She sighed. "Actually, that's not true. I *could* leave," she said, then saw the pleased surprise pass over his face. "But only if I believed that we'd find a home together somewhere else. I won't leave Dallas to wander like a nomad."

"I—"

She shook her head. "No. Don't answer. I've talked about all I can talk today, and now all I can really handle is a bath and a nap. Tomorrow," she

continued, taking his hand and walking him toward
the door, then pressing a kiss to the corner of his
mouth. "You think about what I've said, and I'll see
you at the grand opening tomorrow night." She
brushed his cheek, forcing herself not to cry, and
praying that he wanted her even half as much as she
wanted him. She opened the door, and stepped
through it with him.

"I love you, Ty," she said. "And I'll see you
soon." Then she stepped back inside, closed the
door, and leaned against the heavy oak, hoping like
hell she hadn't made a mistake.

CONSIDERING HOW much he'd managed to cram into
the last twenty-four hours, Ty was amazed that he
actually made it to Heaven's grand opening in
time. He'd had an obscene number of last-minute
errands, not to mention an extraordinary amount of
thinking to do.

He'd even driven by his parents' house in Plano.
He hadn't stopped, but neither had he wrecked his
car or been overcome by a desire to flee the country,
so he considered the journey a success.

And, of course, he'd been making a few final,
special arrangements. For one thing, he'd enlisted
Matt's help, after explaining the situation to his

friend. "The ball's in your court now," Matt had said. "Don't blow it."

When Ty had explained he was trying to not do exactly that, Matt had agreed to set himself up as stand-in bachelor material, subject to winner Alicia Barksley's approval. Fortunately, Alicia was a romantic, who appreciated the story Ty told. More than that, though, she liked the limousine and the stand-in.

So that, at least, had worked out well.

But the rest? The part that involved Claire? Never once had it occurred to Ty that she wouldn't be home, and now he felt like an idiot standing in front of a house with a limo behind him.

"Idiot." Of course, was what he was, and as soon as he saw Claire, he intended to make certain that she knew he realized it.

In the meantime, he had to get to the opening, and after sticking a note for Claire between the frame and the door, he headed back to the limousine and poured himself a Scotch. Considering the crowd he would be speaking to tonight— considering what he was going to say—he needed all the help he could get.

When he arrived, Heaven looked fabulous. His staff had done an amazing job, and the signage colors seemed to leap off the building and into the dark, giving the place a celestial glow.

*Beautiful,* especially with the soft glow of the full moon shining down on them.

He only wished Claire were there to see it with him.

His eyes scanned the crowd waiting to enter the club, but he didn't find her, and the weight of loneliness settled on him. How many of these had he done by himself? He didn't know, but now, it felt like he couldn't continue without her by his side.

The podium, however, was set up, and it was almost showtime. He really had no choice.

Slowly, the limo traveled up the narrow service driveway, and Ty emerged to a wild round of applause.

He held up his hands, both in acknowledgment and to make them stop, and after a few minutes, the crowd calmed.

"Don't let the podium and the crowd fool you," he said, as the press conference began. "I'm going to be brief, because I know that most of you are here for one reason, and one reason only—to get inside and dance."

A raucous cheer rose from the crowd, and he let his eyes survey the group once again. Still no Claire.

"But first, I want to tell you about a very special woman. Some of you have probably already seen pictures of her—and if so, well, you know how beautiful she is," he added wryly. "But what you may not know is who she is. Her name is Claire," he said simply. "And she's the woman I love."

This time, when he searched the crowd, he did find her. Her eyes were bright with surprise, and her mouth was slightly parted, as if she wanted to tell him something, and didn't know how to put it into words. Around her, a small group stepped back, looking at her, rather than him.

"Claire," he said. "I'm sorry. And I love you."

*I love you,* she replied, mouthing the words and setting the nearby group to cheer.

"Things change when you're in love," Ty continued. "Some of you may know that I'm in the process of developing a number of internationally based clubs. And that plan is still in effect, but I'm going to be delegating more to my team. Traveling less. It's important to me that I stay home now. And this is home. Right here. Dallas." He drew in a breath. "My hometown."

A hush had fallen over the crowd, but Claire could hear a faint throbbing noise. After a moment, she realized it was the beating of her own heart.

"And in case any of you think I'm not serious," he added, though his eyes were only on her, "I put a deposit down on a house today. That's not to say I have to live there, or even that I have to buy it, but the wheels are in motion. Frankly, I think I already have a home in Dallas. But I guess I'll have to wait and see on that."

She nodded, just one tiny tilt of her chin, but he noticed, and his smile bloomed wide.

*Home.*

He was staying home. With her.

*He loved her.*

"Claire Daniels," he said into the microphone. "This club is dedicated to you. Because I didn't know heaven until I met you." He found her eyes, held them. "I love you. Now will you come cut the ribbon?"

The request surprised her, but the people nearby were more than happy to urge her forward. She reached the podium, and Ty reached out, doing nothing more than brushing the tips of his fingers over her hand. It was enough to melt her.

"You're really staying?" she whispered.

"I'm really staying."

"Why?"

"Because I love you. And because this is home."

"But your childhood. Your parents."

He lifted a shoulder. "Nuisances. It's home," he added, firmly. "It's home, because you're here."

She wanted to melt under his words, but instead let him help her stand steady.

Then he passed her the scissors, and as the crowd applauded like crazy, she cut the tape that blocked the front door, then stepped aside to let the crowd move in, right into Ty's waiting arms.

"You're sure?"

"I've never been more sure," he said. "Although I'll confess I don't want the house I put the deposit on. I have a different place in mind. It's got these really great stained concrete floors."

She laughed. "That's a popular place, but I have an in with the owner. I bet we can accommodate you."

"Good."

"You could have just talked to me alone," she said. "You didn't have to do this. In front of everybody, I mean. You told the whole world about us."

"Is that bad?"

She thought about it and shook her head. "No."

"Good. Because I needed the world to know that you're mine. And," he added, before brushing a kiss across her lips, "that I'm yours, too. I love you, Claire," he said. "And I always will."

Then, as the crowd applauded and cameras flashed, he kissed her, hard, under the soft glow of a shining, full moon.

And that, thought Claire, was one for the blogs.

* * * * *

*Fan favorite Leslie Kelly is bringing her readers a
fantasy so scandalous,
we're calling it FORBIDDEN!*

*Look for
PLAY WITH ME
Available February 2010 from Harlequin® Blaze™.*

"Aren't you going to say 'Fly me' or at least
'Welcome Aboard'?"

Amanda Bauer didn't. The softly muttered word
that actually came out of her mouth was a lot less
welcoming. And had fewer letters. Four, to be exact.

The man shook his head and tsked. "Not exactly
the friendly skies. Haven't caught the spirit yet
this morning?"

"Make one more airline-slogan crack and you'll
be walking to Chicago," she said.

He nodded once, then pushed his sunglasses onto
the top of his tousled hair. The move revealed blue
eyes that matched the sky above. And, yeah. They
were twinkling. Dammit.

"Understood. Just, uh, promise me you'll say
'Coffee, tea or me' at least once, okay? Please?"

Amanda tried to glare, but that twinkle sucked the

annoyance right out of her. She could only draw in a slow breath as he climbed into the plane. As she watched her passenger disappear into the small jet, she had to wonder about the trip she was about to take.

Coffee and tea they had, and he was welcome to them. But her? Well, she'd never even considered making a move on a customer before. Talk about unprofessional.

And yet…

Something inside her suddenly wanted to take a chance, to be a little outrageous.

How long since she had done indecent things—or decent ones, for that matter—with a sexy man? Not since before they'd thrown all their energies into expanding Clear-Blue Air, at the very least. She hadn't had time for a lunch date, much less the kind of lust-fest she'd enjoyed in her younger years. The kind that lasted for entire weekends and involved not leaving a bed except to grab the kind of sensuous food that could be smeared onto—and eaten off—someone else's hot, naked, sweat-tinged body.

She closed her eyes, her hand clenching tight on the railing. Her heart fluttered in her chest and she tried to make herself move. But she couldn't—not climbing up, but not backing away, either. Not physically, and not in her head.

Was she really considering this? God, she hadn't even looked at the stranger's left hand to make sure he was available. She had no idea if he was actually attracted to her or just an irrepressible flirt. Yet something inside was telling her to take a shot with this man.

It was crazy. Something she'd never considered. Yet right now, at this moment, she was definitely considering it. If he was available…could she do it? Seduce a stranger. Have an anonymous fling, like something out of a blue movie on late-night cable?

She didn't know. All she knew was that the flight to Chicago was a short one so she had to decide quickly. And as she put her foot on the bottom step and began to climb up, Amanda suddenly had to wonder if she was about to embark on the ride of her life.

# HARLEQUIN® Blaze™

## *Do you have a forbidden fantasy?*

Amanda Bauer does. She's always craved a life
of adventure…sexual adventure, that is. And
when she meets Reese Campbell, she knows he's
just the man to play with. And play they do. Every
few months they get together for days of wild sex,
no strings attached—or so they think….

### Sneak away with:

# Play with Me

## by LESLIE KELLY

*Available February 2010
wherever Harlequin books are sold.*

---

# red-hot reads

**Stay up-to-date on all your romance-reading news with the brand-new Harlequin *Inside Romance!***

The Harlequin *Inside Romance* is a **FREE** quarterly newsletter highlighting our upcoming series releases and promotions!

Click on the *Inside Romance* link on the front page of **www.eHarlequin.com** or e-mail us at InsideRomance@Harlequin.ca to sign up to receive your **FREE** newsletter today!

You can also subscribe by writing to us at: HARLEQUIN BOOKS
Attention: Customer Service Department
P.O. Box 9057, Buffalo, NY 14269-9057

*Please allow 4-6 weeks for delivery of the first issue by mail.*

IRNBPAQ309

HARLEQUIN *Presents*

Sold, bought, bargained for or bartered

*He'll take his…*

# *Bride on Approval*

Whether there's a debt to be paid,
a will to be obeyed or a business
to be saved…she has no choice
but to say, "I do"!

# PURE PRINCESS, BARTERED BRIDE
### by *Caitlin Crews*
#### *#2894*

*Available February 2010!*

# REQUEST YOUR FREE BOOKS!

## 2 FREE NOVELS PLUS 2 FREE GIFTS!

HARLEQUIN®

*Blaze*

Red-hot reads!

**YES!** Please send me 2 FREE Harlequin® Blaze™ novels and my 2 FREE gifts (gifts are worth about $10). After receiving them, if I don't wish to receive any more books, I can return the shipping statement marked "cancel." If I don't cancel, I will receive 6 brand-new novels every month and be billed just $4.24 per book in the U.S. or $4.71 per book in Canada. That's a saving of close to 15% off the cover price. It's quite a bargain. Shipping and handling is just 50¢ per book in the U.S. and 75¢ per book in Canada.* I understand that accepting the 2 free books and gifts places me under no obligation to buy anything. I can always return a shipment and cancel at any time. Even if I never buy another book, the two free books and gifts are mine to keep forever.

151 HDN E4CY   351 HDN E4CN

| | |
|---|---|
| Name | (PLEASE PRINT) |
| Address | Apt. # |
| City | State/Prov.   Zip/Postal Code |

Signature (if under 18, a parent or guardian must sign)

### Mail to the Harlequin Reader Service:
**IN U.S.A.:** P.O. Box 1867, Buffalo, NY 14240-1867
**IN CANADA:** P.O. Box 609, Fort Erie, Ontario L2A 5X3

Not valid for current subscribers to Harlequin Blaze books.

**Want to try two free books from another line?
Call 1-800-873-8635 or visit www.morefreebooks.com.**

\* Terms and prices subject to change without notice. Prices do not include applicable taxes. N.Y. residents add applicable sales tax. Canadian residents will be charged applicable provincial taxes and GST. Offer not valid in Quebec. This offer is limited to one order per household. All orders subject to approval. Credit or debit balances in a customer's account(s) may be offset by any other outstanding balance owed by or to the customer. Please allow 4 to 6 weeks for delivery. Offer available while quantities last.

**Your Privacy:** Harlequin Books is committed to protecting your privacy. Our Privacy Policy is available online at www.eHarlequin.com or upon request from the Reader Service. From time to time we make our lists of customers available to reputable third parties who may have a product or service of interest to you. If you would prefer we not share your name and address, please check here. ☐

**Help us get it right**—We strive for accurate, respectful and relevant communications. To clarify or modify your communication preferences, visit us at www.ReaderService.com/consumerchoice.

# HARLEQUIN

## *Ambassadors*

### *Want to share your passion for reading Harlequin® Books?*

## Become a Harlequin Ambassador!

Harlequin Ambassadors are a group of passionate and well-connected readers who are willing to share their joy of reading Harlequin® books with family and friends.

You'll be sent all the tools you need to spark great conversation, including free books!

All we ask is that you share the romance with your friends and family!

You'll also be invited to have a say in new book ideas and exchange opinions with women just like you!

### To see if you qualify* to be a Harlequin Ambassador, please visit **www.HarlequinAmbassadors.com.**

*Please note that not everyone who applies to be a Harlequin Ambassador will qualify. For more information please visit www.HarlequinAmbassadors.com.

**Thank you for your participation.**

BAP09BPA